CONQUEROR OF SHADOW AND LIGHT

MICHAELA BUSH

No AI was used in the creation, research, editing, design, or marketing of this manuscript.
This book is a work of fiction. Names, characters, places, and incidents either are products of the author's imagination or are used fictitiously. Any resemblance to actual persons, living or dead, events, or locales is entirely coincidental.

Michaela Bush

Visit my blog at tangledupinwriting.com

Printed in the United States of America.

First Edition: March 2026

Published through Kindle Direct Publishing, an Amazon Company.

ISBN: 9798988585640

ALSO BY MICHAELA BUSH

Legends of Lanaria

The Lady of Lanaria

The Healer of the Brigade

The Highlander's Victory

The Kingdom's True Queen

The Keeper of the Tower

The Queen of Lanaria

The Legends of Lanaria Special Edition Omnibus: Kindle Edition

The Legends of Lanaria Special Edition Omnibus: Volume One

The Legends of Lanaria Special Edition Omnibus: Volume Two

The Bridge Duology

Back to Me

Between Us

Bethlehem Belle Novellas

Where the Last Verse Ends

Where the Bridge Begins

Where Broken Chords Mend

Standalones

Where Hope Begins

Esperanza: And Other Fantasy Short Stories

Conqueror of Shadow and Light

Faith, Hope, and Love Collection

Faith, Hope, and Love Collection: Volume One

Faith, Hope, and Love Collection: Volume Two

Mount Sterling (out of print)

Beautiful Chaos

Something New

Keeping Cassie

Devotionals

Back To Him: A Thirty Day Devotional on Giving Up Old Hurts and Relying on God

Sustain: A Thirty Day Devotional Dedicated to Remembering God's Sovereignty in Hardship

Rooted: A Thirty-Day Journey through the Prison Epistles

A Dance of Rebels

A Dance of Rebels

Chasing the Lutetia Light

Poetry

Everything I Never Said

Everything And Nothing

everything i became

wading through the fog on a sunny day

hello is goodbye

Contributor

Where Giants Fall (out of print)

Tales From The Tower

Tell Me You Love Me

Seize the Fight (out of print)

The Stars Weep Too

Unleash the Cosmos

Clean Fiction Magazine, Winter 2024 Edition

Snowdrops in Springtime

Unconventional Love

To Love You

Clean Fiction Magazine, Autumn 2025 Edition

Clean Fiction Magazine, Winter 2025 Edition

Dystopians by Makenzie Gray

Those With Ears (Midnight Hour 1)

Let Them Hear (Midnight Hour 2)

Eyes to See (Midnight Hour 3)

Remnant of Us (Midnight Hour 4)

Until Kingdom Come (Midnight Hour 5)

Midnight Hour Omnibus Edition

The Depths We'll Go To **(contributor)**

Here Lies Wanderland **(contributor)**

Then Jesus said to those Jews who believed Him, "If you abide in My word, you are My disciples indeed. And you shall know the truth, and the truth shall make you free." —John 8:31-32

I will give you a new heart and put a new spirit within you; I will take the heart of stone out of your flesh and give you a heart of flesh. — Ezekiel 36:26

THE CURSE

ONE

Cove

Spring's sunlight warred with the foreboding, heavy clouds of winter. Cove kept her eye to the sky as the winds whipped overhead, tangling her unruly brown-black hair that she should've tied back into a braid earlier in the day. This wind, it would churn up a storm sooner rather than later. And she didn't want to be present for it. Tucking into the village hustle-and-bustle, she anticipating the smattering of hail hitting the cobblestones and her head. Yanking her wool cloak hood up for protection, she kept moving against the crowd. Cove wasn't supposed to be in the Black Quarter village anyway, so perhaps the storm was a blessing in disguise: it forced her to conceal her identity. The laws were ridiculous anyway; she only wanted to see her oldest friend. He had been born in the Red Quarter like her, anyway. And no king could stop her.

If he wants to throw me in jail, good. I'm not much longer for this world anyway, according to what everyone says. It came true of her father, the youngest person in Cove's village to die from the stone heart. And it might as well be her fate, too. It was what Grandmother and Mother always said of Cove's temper and attitude toward life. It was as if the deal was done and sealed already. Just a matter of time.

So Cove decided she might as well make it count by breaking rules, as many as she could given such a limited window. Even though this sin against the king should cause the black tendrils weaving up her arms to grow, strangely, it did not. Perhaps because Cove was not bitter when she was seeking Theo. Or perhaps she did not understand the mysterious ways of the curse.

The Black Quarter guards would arrest her and send her back to the Red Quarter if they saw the black patterns adorning her forearms, snaking around her bony elbows and twining up toward her shoulders. Rumor said it was a mark of someone truly wicked, but truth be told, everyone died of it sooner or later. The greatest variable was how long the person lived before they succumbed. The most decent, kind, and generous would live long lives. Others, like Cove's father, passed early in life. The black tendrils reached into his chest, wrapped around his heart, and turned it to stone with his own hot temper. He was twenty-four, and Cove was only six.

She shook aside her thoughts. Now, at seventeen, Mother said that Cove far surpassed Father's own record of misdeeds.

But that's not my fault, Cove mentally retorted as she rushed against the crowd, head bent, curls obscuring her face. *My father's blood runs through my veins just as much as hers do, and the black tendrils are reaching past Mother's shoulders and collarbone, stretching for her heart, too.* It was only a matter of time for her.

Grandmother was the only one who only had the mark of the curse on her forearms. She might stand a chance at a full life, unless sickness or murder took her. It was the fate assigned to everyone in Solmere. If the stone heart didn't take a person, some twisted design of nature or hatred would take care of it. Perhaps it was the same way across the world, if Cove only knew.

She could travel, if she had the chance. See if some of the world was truly good or just as divided and hateful as Solmere. But when the tendrils reached her heart, it would turn to stone. No use adventuring when fates end the same.

It was as simple as that.

Cove snatched the cloak closer around her torso, careful to hide even her fingers—for the tendrils vined around her fingers, too, like ornate rings of fortune—as she kept moving.

"Hey! Red Quarter! What are you doing?"

Cove picked up the pace as a guard addressed her sharply. Better to pretend she could not hear. In the Black Quarter, there were mainly the sickly, disabled, the deaf and blind and crippled. It wouldn't be a shock if someone didn't hear him. Maybe he would believe he saw wrong.

TWO

THEO

A COMMOTION ROSE SOME yards away from Theo. Many pairs of feet scattered away from the commanding voice.

"Red Quarter, answer me! What are you doing here?"

Theo didn't catch the voice that answered the guard, much as he strained to hear. It couldn't be Cove. His palms slicked with sweat. *Not Cove, too. Don't let her be caught...* He wasn't sure who his thoughts ascended to, but he only hoped they were heard. It was too often Theo's fault that harm came; he couldn't lose her too.

But he was sitting there at the corner of the busy Black Quarter village, helpless despite his most desperate urge to rescue Cove—or whoever was in the line of questioning. But as a Black Quarter man, Theo couldn't do anything, much less defy a guard. A crippled man to his left, whose name he'd never learned, moaned.

"Are you well?" Theo asked. Working his own foot backward, he bumped the crippled man's shin so he knew Theo was there.

"They'll take it out on us," he said, voice gravelly, and he settled to murmuring it to himself over and over. As if Theo didn't already know. The scar across his cheekbone burned as if it had just happened.

"Maybe not this time," Theo whispered, though he couldn't deny the wheedling tone he'd taken on.

"Sure." The crippled man fell silent and Theo heard scraping, as if he'd begun dragging himself away on his elbows. *He's had enough of me, too,* Theo thought.

A sudden chill came to rest in the crippled man's place, and Theo didn't even have someone to tell him what was going on. Normally, there was someone, somewhere. But when even Theo's own family wouldn't have much to do with him, why expect a stranger to?

The Black Quarter's cursed relied on themselves.

The Red Quarter's cursed relied on themselves.

As far as he knew, the other Quarters kept to themselves, too. And never the twain shall meet.

It was the way of the world. Those gifted with normality, with some sense of capability, were able to keep themselves away from the most impoverished, and those without the worst tempers or disablements were divided up either in the Gray or the Gold Quarters. All the others were left to suffer and die, branded burdens by Solmere.

It wasn't always this way. Some centuries ago, a prophet came proclaiming that the way of peace was coming. But something ancient rose up and consumed the weeping prophet, and now they only had death and decay.

Suppose the prophet was wrong, then.

Theo shifted his weight from tailbone to legs and feet, then guided himself down the road as the commotion continued on, this time softer. Farther away. Someone slammed into Theo's shoulder and kept moving, shouting at Theo to keep to himself.

"Same to you," Theo halfheartedly snapped, but it came out...lacking. What was he going to do in retaliation, exactly?

Theo's hands trailed a doorframe, a windowsill, then open air. The blacksmith's, by the acrid smoke drifting through the breeze. The baker was some yards down and had just pulled an apple pie from the flames, by the way Theo's mouth watered in response to the sweet scent wafting past. Even the odors of work and human misery surrounding him couldn't squelch that simple pleasure. When was the last time Theo had a pie? Perhaps before Mother decided to obey Father and leave him on the doorstep of the Quarter's captain of the guard, typical for orphans or families who were giving up their child due to a curse.

It had been thirteen years—since Theo was four years old—that he was instructed by the captain to stay out of everyone's way. He'd led Theo by the hand and told him everything: which corners of the town were reserved for beggars, and what would become of Theo if he disobeyed any of the contrived rules ordered down by Solmere's king.

What Theo would never understand, though, is how he was cursed to begin with...and why nothing could be done to lift the burden. If not for others who tried and failed to care for Theo, but also for himself. If the king despised the burdensome, wouldn't he try to find a way to ensure they were able to care for themselves, instead of simply shunning them all? Some, with strange maladies of the mind or nervousness, were able to live peaceably and hold their own as shepherds or bakers. The blacksmith was deaf, but capable of running his own business. Others, like the cripple, would always need help in one way or another. And there shouldn't be anything disrespectful about that; it wasn't his choice.

It wasn't mine, either.

None of the Black Quarter villagers would choose this life of reliance, of asking for help and swallowing nonexistent pride, of being kicked by those careless toward their conditions. But despite all those who despised the Black Quarter villagers, there were a few cracks of sunlight allowed in.

Theo's sliver of sunlight was Cove. Though she was a Red Quarter and not permitted to cross over, she remembered Theo from before his parents gave him up to the Black Quarter. Cove and Theo were neighbors, playmates. She would guide him around the yard, teaching him what trees looked like and paired description to the birdsong he loved listening to. What Theo's own family looked like, even. And ever since her father showed her the Black Quarter, she made a habit of sneaking over and describing to Theo what was going on in the Black Quarter. Sometimes, she would shove a warm bun and, even rarer, a lump of cheese into Theo's palms. She would always fill his tin cup with fresh water, and then she would rush off, a ghost in the breeze.

Theo would give anything to see her face.

But right now, he had to make sure she was all right and not harmed by the guard.

Moving faster, Theo broke out into a clumsy jog, relying on the stone buildings flanking the streets—that is, until he tripped over someone, or something, and fell face first, skidding what felt like a meter before painfully grinding to a halt.

"What do we have here?"

A guard, Theo presumed, based on the authoritative, harsh voice.

"Theo, Black Quarter. I belong here. My apologies. I didn't see. I can't—that is, I can't see. My apologies, sir." Theo pulled himself up to his knees and bowed his head, hoping he was facing the man. From the laugh aimed at his back, Theo decided otherwise. The guard was behind him—had probably tripped him, too. Shame ripped through Theo, and blood prickled as it reached the surface of his skinned palms.

Theo swallowed the tears of embarrassment that built in the back of his throat. "I heard a commotion."

"Black Quarter..." He added a few slurs that turned Theo's tears into rage.

But he couldn't do anything. Theo started to rise silently, but a solid hand slammed into his chest, knocking him flat on his back.

"Where do you think you're going? You *assaulted* me," the guard spat.

If Cove was there, she was not responding. *Not good.*

Theo's heart began to hammer.

THREE

Cove

"Let go of me!" Cove snarled. She threw her full body weight against the guard seizing her arm, and when that didn't work, slammed her head backward.

Crunch.

She and the man screamed as their skulls connected. Blood sprayed against her neck from his nose. His grip only tightened.

"I'll cut your throat for that, Red Quarter," he hissed in her ear.

"Good!" she snapped, then bit down on his arm and kicked backwards, going first for the groin and then the shins.

She couldn't cry for help. No one would come. She wasn't meant to be here. Wasn't meant to be seen. The guard snarled and shoved her into an alley, slamming her into a stone wall.

"I'll make you regret—"

"Stop!" a commanding voice spoke. It wasn't a shout, nor a snarl like so many of the guards spoke with. But it held an authority that sent a chill into Cove's core. Something inside her shrank from the man, and her veins burned.

"Get away from me!" the guard shrieked. He must have felt the same thing. Suddenly, he clutched his temples and doubled over, letting Cove go as he moaned in pain. He stumbled away two steps.

Cove glanced between the stranger and the guard.

The stranger's eyes were clearer than any she'd ever seen, a brown that could expand for centuries within their depths. His face wasn't unkind, just firm.

The guard fell to the ground and crawled on his hands and knees.

Cove glanced over to the guard and landed a kick just for good measure, then ran down the alleyway. Toward the stranger—which wasn't a splendid choice, but her only option for escape.

"Are you well?" the stranger asked, holding out an arm to stop her.

"Yes. Let me go. Please. I know I'm not supposed to be here, just let me go home!" she begged. Panic tightened her chest.

"Of course." He turned on his heel and, with long strides, kept apace. Panic edged through her chest. "I'll accompany you to the border."

So, was he a guard in commoner clothes? Cove shook her head, confused. "I can get there myself." She still had to get to Theo. But with this man...maybe it was better to not try anything. She rubbed at her veins, the black stains that worked their way up her wrists, forearms, shoulders. Were they growing? Is that why her chest ached?

Was *it* going to happen today?

Sweat prickled out of her flesh, cold and damp across her forehead. She didn't want to die just yet, with no meaning in her legacy. What would happen to Theo?

The stranger cast a glance toward her. "I could help you with those. I know of a cure. It's not a curse, by the way. Neither is your friend cursed for being blind."

How does he know about Theo? How does he know about me? She recoiled. "How do you—"

"It looks like we're at the border," the stranger said, breaking her off. "Like I said, I know a cure. My name is Iosua if you wish to find me. I promise you would be made whole."

"I *am* whole," Cove snapped. "I don't know who you are, but clairvoyants don't belong in the Black Quarter."

He chuckled softly. "I don't belong anywhere, it seems. But if you ask for me, you will find me. Before something happens to you or your friend, I would recommend."

She shook her head, muttering about the insane man, and broke into a run for her house. The Black Quarter disappeared, and she crawled under a barbed wire fence that served as the divider between quarters. She caught her dress and her cloak on it, and she carefully extricated herself so as to not tear the cloak. It had been a gift from her mother. She wouldn't destroy it for this strange man. She half-expected him to be following her, but after she wriggled under the dividing fence, she cast a glance behind her. The man had disappeared.

Uncertainty prickled her skin and her veins stopped burning as soon as she got away from him.

She tore through the woods, hopping downed branches and brambles, aimed in the most direct route to her home. Panting, Cove barreled into the house she, her mother, and grandmother shared, slamming the door shut. Her chest heaved as she leaned against the door.

"Don't slam that door, you know the hinges are 'bout to fall apart," her grandmother snapped harshly.

"Good morning to you, too." Cove wheezed. "I was attacked by a guard and then this strange man...followed me to the border."

"Border of where?" her mother asked, appearing from the kitchen and wiping her hands, narrowing her eyes at her daughter. "You know you shouldn't associate with Theo. Not with your current state of affairs. Don't ruin this for us *or* yourself."

Cove's stomach twisted as she glanced across the cramped living area toward a brown-paper wrapped parcel that Mother jerked her head toward. "It arrived?"

"Yes. Erik's servants were hoping to return with word from you, but I told them you were on errands for me. You're lucky this time. I might not lie next time. Go open it up, see what you've got for the betrothal ball. You really ought to be practicing your dances, and I don't understand why Erik didn't bring you to the manor for lessons. We all know he's got no morals to defend." Her voice was harsh, gravelly, and she smirked darkly as she swung away and headed back for the kitchen. "Unless you're going to throw everything away for the blind boy."

"No! Of course not." Cove cleared her throat, overly aware of her grandmother seated on the rocking chair, staring daggers at her. Her face wasn't flushed...at least, she hoped not. "I want this, Mother. I want to be Erik's betrothed. It will bring you and Grandmother honor."

It was a bald-faced lie, but one she told herself to keep her own sanity. Her father's death meant he couldn't secure betrothal himself. Even if he had been alive, any arrangement he could have sorted out wouldn't have been so advantageous to the family...and with his death, responsibility rested squarely on Cove's shoulders. Even if she died, the dowry would help her mother and grandmother.

Three months prior, when Cove had been—again—sneaking near the dividing corner that split all four Quarters, the royal procession had gone through on their twice-yearly parade. Proving to the Quarters how powerless they were, by Cove's estimation. The king's son, Erik, had passed through on his white mare and she'd caught his eye. That's what the servant said when he'd sent word requesting her presence the following day. She didn't know how they'd found her cottage. But she did understand the servant's demands.

The four Quarters typically offered up their virgins for the king's lesser children—the four boys who would *not* ascend to the throne—in order to keep the peace amongst the Quarters. After the first marriage, the princes could select as many concubines as they so desired, but a handsome dowry was offered for the first. So Prince Erik was her future. And she should have been thrilled.

She unwrapped the parcel and fingered the crimson silk ballgown. Its capped sleeves would cut short just above her stains, showcasing them. Erik loved them, he said. But did he realize this curse would kill her? Perhaps before she brought forth children for him. She shuddered at the thought of carrying his children. She wasn't certain how Erik had survived this long, but something wicked was certainly involved. She'd caught a glance at King Lycidas on that day three months ago. His skin, normally tan by her estimation, was completely covered in shades of black. No intricate pattern along his veins—just pure darkness. He wore a bulky onyx crown that looked as heavy as it did imposing, and etched in it were images of Solmere idols. And on the first day Erik had formally met with Cove, he had assured her there was a plan afoot to topple his father's reign.

"You'll wear that crown one day, Cove," he had said, tipping her chin up as if measuring her up. He'd patted her cheek with a gaze devoid of light. "As long as you do as I expect."

Her thoughts veered away from the man who would soon own her. Iosua had a plan to conquer the curse, eh?

Perhaps she should seek him out and get the cure before her marriage; some sort of gift for Erik. A peace treaty, since she couldn't see a way out of marrying him now. Would Iosua help Theo, too? Once she was married, she wouldn't be able to help him anymore.

She swallowed hard and shoved the parcel closed again. No. She needed to put such notions out of her head once and for all. She slammed her mind shut on the mysterious man.

But her mind wouldn't shut a door on Theo, no matter how hard she tried.

FOUR

THEO

MOLD PINCHED HIS NOSE and hard, damp stone bit into his shoulder, but he couldn't move. His hands were bound behind his back. Still, he inched his way onto his belly until his head bumped into the opposing wall. So he was in a cell. Metal on metal clanged, and something slammed down. Something wet sloshed on Theo's ankles and he jerked away.

"Eat," a man's voice demanded.

"I can't," Theo said. "I'm bound—"

"Figure it out, cursed rat," the voice responded, cutting him off short. The metal-on-metal clanged again, shutting Theo off from the world.

In the close distance, the interaction was repeated with Theo's next-door neighbor.

Theo inched his way toward his ankles, carefully drawing his knees up to his chest and wriggling to get his arms to the front of him instead of being trapped behind. Then, fumbling, he searched for the tray that had been thrown on the ground.

If prison meant food until he was executed, perhaps it wasn't a bad lot. It would be an interesting way to die. A simpler, more merciful way than what most Black Quarters experienced.

Although he wasn't sure why he'd been captured, aside from whatever lie the guard had conjured about Theo attacking him.

Without being able to see his own arms, he couldn't tell how far-progressed his sin stains were. He really only knew about it because of Cove's descriptions anyway. Had the curse almost run its course with him? Surely he wouldn't get out alive this time—either by the stone heart or by execution.

His fingers found stale bread, and he carefully fed himself every last crumb. It wasn't nearly as good as the bread Cove brought. But it was food. In his fumbling attempt to find the cup of water, he spilled it over into the tray, and lowered himself to slurp it out of the tray, lapping it dry. It had been too long since he'd had fresh water. Though it didn't exactly taste fresh.

A scream reached his ears, and he tensed, face pressed to the tray. A scuffling of shoes, louder and then softer as the screaming man and at least two other pairs of boots marched past. A door slammed and he jolted, chest sparking with fear. The screams, though faint, could still be heard—and then they cut off short. He grimaced, and men began to shout in the distance.

"He was an innocent!"

"Death to the king!"

"Death to the Quarters!"

"Death to Prince Erik and his brothers!"

Such a ruckus erupted that Theo shrugged his shoulders up to his ears, trying to muffle the insanity. A guard came in, screamed a demand for silence, and everyone ceased.

Unease crawled through Theo's throat. Hadn't he, just a few minutes prior, felt like this was a gift? To die here instead of on the streets?

What if he really did? Fear crawled across his chest, sparked alive in his stomach, and grew deeper, reaching its roots for his heart.

Maybe this really was it. And he wasn't even sure what had happened to Cove yesterday.

FIVE

Cove

Cove ran. Feet beating on the cobblestones, kicking a chicken out of the way, shoving past merchants and beggars alike, ignoring the need to keep her cloak's hood over her face and curls.

"Stop!" a guard commanded. She didn't cast a backwards glance.

Rage burned her chest. She ran straight through the intersection between Red and Black Quarters, not slowing until she saw the tall manor that would one day be hers.

It had rattled her far more than she'd expected, finding Theo's spot vacant this morning. The cripple who typically sat with him had crawled over and tugged her skirt.

"They took him, girl. Go away before they find you, too." Then he'd held his hands out expectantly for the bread Cove had tucked inside her cloak.

Which was fine. Cove had dropped it without a second thought. And then she began to run.

She would have been faster on horseback, but there were few in the Red or Black Quarters. They only kept animals that were readily eaten and easily kept in small, cramped, fenced-in areas—chickens or sheep.

She reached the manor gates and stopped, composing herself for a moment before the guard could turn her way.

"I'm here to see Erik," she said, straightening her shoulders and holding her chin high lest the guard question her. It had happened on more than one occasion in the past three months. And it irked her each time.

The guard, in silver and black armor, looked at her askance. "For?"

"I'm his betrothed, must I disclose every jot and tittle we share?" Cove asked sharply.

The man shook his head and swung the gate wide, arching a brow. "This way. But he's in a tutoring intensive."

"Then summon him. It's an emergency." After the guard left to do as she'd asked, Cove shook her head. Only the wealthiest could be tutored. She hardly knew how to read, aside from signs that would mean life or death to her. Her parents said ignorance kept her safe; it was a good excuse to use against the guards. Faux stupidity went so far. But then fate wound up reversed, once in awhile, and someone ended up at the end of a rope.

But it worked just now, and she sucked in a deep breath. She was ushered quickly to the sitting-room, where she refused to sit. Erik would have a fit of rage if she muddied the pure-white and gold fabrics covering the room. Still, a grayness pervaded every corner that shocked Cove no matter how many times she entered Erik's manor. A *heaviness.* It was meant to be beautiful. Light, pure, and soft. But it only felt suffocating to her.

Even more so now, but that was because Theo was missing and in prison, where he wouldn't survive. And she was certain he had done nothing wrong.

The prisons were glorified torture facilities; everyone knew that, especially and including the nobility. A blind boy wouldn't be able to fight back. And she knew Theo was too pure-hearted to do anything worth imprisonment. Most times, the others imprisoned were at least there for a very good reason. Murder. Theft. Matters even more heinous that sent a shiver down Cove's spine. Typically, the prisons hardened their hearts even further until they died from the curse before their sentencing even came up. If the sentencing came up, it would be the noose.

Theo's arms were the cleanest Cove had ever seen. Only little tendrils of black on his fingertips, the longest stain working to his wrist and stopping there. From an offense when he was a very small boy, no doubt. Theo didn't deserve such treatment.

Cove did. Most of the people she knew did.

Erik did, no doubt.

But not Theo.

"My sprite, what is it?" Erik's baritone preceded him as he appeared in the doorway, something clouding his face. Annoyance. "Is the dress not to your—"

Cove shook her head. "I haven't seen the dress yet, I'm sure it's fine. I'm here because a man has been wrongfully detained in prison. You have the authority to reverse their decision and set him free."

Erik's thick brown brows knit together, and he glanced over Cove from top to bottom and back. "Who is this man to you?" He tilted his head, watching intently for her response.

"I-I only see him at the corner, and he wasn't there and his neighbor was terrified for me, so I ran and—" Cove's lie spun out of her control and dropped on the floor like a spool of unkept thread. How could she explain without giving the appearance of concern? To admit she'd been in the Black Quarter would criminalize herself.

Erik smirked and shook his head. "Little sprite, you don't need to worry yourself with the commoners any more. Soon, you'll be in the Gold Quarter where you belong and they won't matter. Don't worry your little head, I'm sure he deserves to be there."

Cove's hands fisted together. "You don't know that."

"Don't I?" His gaze turned scrutinizing. "Cove, I won't despise you for the life you led before accepting my betrothal. The animals in Black and Red have to do what they must to survive. But you are expected to maintain an image now. Let go of the past and seize the future. You will be feared soon enough. Begin acting so, or the commoners will destroy you. I told you, you'll wear my father's crown someday. Along with me. It has been prophesied by my father's priests—in secret, of course. To say so against him would be treachery."

Theo was no *animal.* Her family wasn't, either. Her fingernails bit into her palms. And she didn't fool herself with so-called prophecies made by liars. Or anyone, really.

Cove's gaze flickered to Erik's hands, which fisted much like her own. Black stained his fingers, twisted around his arms in a chain of vines, and disappeared beneath his sleeve at the elbow. His blood pumped angrily in their own veins beneath the surface, especially at his neck, where the stains reappeared from his shirt collar.

How far did his stains go? Cove wondered. Perhaps he would die before her. It shamed her to feel relief at the notion. But she knew he was a short-tempered man, and those fists had sent holes in the walls before—which he'd laughed off and said his father would simply send an architect to repair and improve the wall for him.

"I am simply concerned about a good citizen." She forced herself to speak levelly. Calmly. She'd seen her mother use the same tactic with her father when he was in a mood.

But Erik's expression darkened. "Cove. You aren't talking about that blind boy, are you? My men see you with him from time to time. Let it go. Or else that same curse will be laid upon our children too, and what would the people think of a blind son of a royal?" He scoffed, face darkening. "Let that be your final warning. I need to return to my business, and I think you should too. Don't forget the betrothal ball two weeks hence. You got the dress?"

"Yes," Cove answered curtly. So she was Cove now, spoken with a sharpness, not his *little sprite.* The same nickname he gave her upon their first meeting. He'd lowered a hand from his white mare, beckoning her to come close. She'd hesitated, but decided it was better to acknowledge the nobility than ignore him entirely; to do so would have been a death sentence. *"Little sprite, to whom do you belong? If a ring doesn't rest on your finger, why not allow me to stake my claim?"* He'd charmed until he got his way, and then he quit the act and showed his true form.

Face burning with anger, Cove stormed out of the manor, ignoring the guards' shouts. Who cared what they thought? She had to get someone to help Theo. And since she would be Erik's prize soon enough, it would be her authority to release him from prison. As his betrothed, that authority may as well rest upon her. Right? If she could just lie better than she had before...

She took a deep breath and plunged headlong into her race back to Theo. Or where he *should* have been.

As she skidded, breathless and wheezing, for the corner she knew so well, a voice materialized at her side. "You again? What's the rush?"

She spun around. Iosua. A shudder worked through her. "Don't do that. Why are you in the Black Quarter, anyway?

You're not ill. They'll kill you if they catch you." She shook her head. "Never mind. I can't tarry."

"You're trying to help your friend. Yes?"

The stranger's words stopped her in her tracks. Again with the knowledge that frightened her so deeply. She backed up, eyes wide and heart thundering. "You know too much. Get away from me. I don't associate with seers."

"No. I saw them taking him, and I knew you'd be upset. Don't be afraid." He held his hands out, and Cove's gaze darted quickly to them, assessing the threat. They were browned and calloused from hard, manual labor, but empty. Not clenched in anger. Just open. "I can help you."

"How? The nobility won't, and you...you're not nobility. No offense."

A grin quirked his mouth beneath his scraggly brown beard. "No. Not in this world, and not in your life. But nobility has its own shortfalls, and I believe you know that too. I also know a man named Rune who is aware of when the guard change happens at the jail. We can release Theo with little fuss, no violence. It would be safer for him."

"I was going to force them into releasing him by using Erik's name." She paused, touching her fingers to her lips. "I suppose I shouldn't have said that. I am his betrothed."

He nodded, his smile turning somewhat forced. "I know. Rumor spreads fast. Cove, yes? Is this a pleasant blessing for you?"

She nodded as well, and then his gaze flicked to her arms. Her cloak had slipped, revealing a new tendril shooting up toward her shoulder. It seared, and she couldn't tell whether it was thanks to his gaze alone, or the burning of her heart growing harder and harder to stone.

"He never listens to me," she muttered brusquely, fixing her cloak with haste. "Don't worry about it. You say you can help me rescue Theo?"

"Yes." Iosua paused, then took a deep breath. "Erik is wrong about a good many things. And I believe helping you with Theo will prove a few things to you, too. I need you, and Theo and a few others, for something in the coming days."

She scoffed. "You ought to look in different kingdoms if you want useful help. Look around you. We're a dying people."

"Yes. But I want to save the lost and dying. I believe this curse has to end. Don't you?"

Cove's brow furrowed. "Doesn't seem like your responsibility, nor your area of expertise. It would take an incredible sacrifice to cure every last cursed person in Solmere alone."

Iosua nodded slowly. "Well, then. We can start one person at a time...and I think you'd agree Theo is that one. Yes? Then follow me."

She did so without a second thought, though her heart raced. Who was he—and who did he think he was? Was he involved with Erik's plan to overturn King Lycidas? Or was this an uprising? Gooseflesh prickled up across her arms as she considered the possibility.

SIX

THEO

RETREATING FOOTSTEPS ALLOWED THEO a moment to breathe. How long had it been? A day? A week? A few hours? He couldn't tell by the sun's waning and strengthening warmth, nor the foot traffic. He imagined mealtimes would be sporadic, probably based on the guards—which ones were compassionate enough to keep the prisoners alive. He didn't even have his neighbors in the Black Quarter to tell him what was going on around him. But he knew one thing, and it was that when the boots were angling away from him, he was better off.

A soft scuff caught his ear, and he tipped his head to the left. Listening. Wondering. It wasn't the purposeful stride of someone who belonged there. A quiet clank.

Quietly, he scrambled until he could back himself into the corner. The harsh, cold stone felt comforting against his back; at least no one could sneak up from behind. It offered solidity. Protection.

"Shh. It's Cove," a familiar voice hissed.

Theo froze.

It sounded like her.

Shoving aside his confusion, he reached out and moved toward the bars, then slipped his hand through and found her hand with his.

She squeezed it tight. "Quickly, now," she whispered.

He squeezed her hand so she knew he'd heard, then stepped back. A quiet screech from the hinges suggested the bars were swinging open. Another arm came from Theo's other side and wrapped around his shoulders, someone taller and broader than Cove. Callouses brushed against his thin shirt from the person's palm. He didn't say a word for the time being, he only focused on matching his pace with the stranger and Cove's.

"There are steps." The stranger's voice was low, belonging to a man.

Huh—a man with Cove? Theo furrowed his brows, but nodded and lifted his right foot cautiously, feeling for the stone lip. And then the next and the next, as fast as he could possibly move. And then the sun shone on his face again.

But the other two didn't slow or cease their forward movement, so he didn't either. Not until the sounds and smells hit Theo's stomach as home. Back to his Quarter. And he'd never realized how much he appreciated the inhumanity of the Black Quarter until now—wretched or not, it was still *life*. The sun could shine on him. He could see with his ears, thanks to the others willing to speak to him. Not the isolation that proved to be prison.

It was only after he could smell the bakery that he spoke. "Who is this man, Cove?"

"Iosua," the man supplied.

"Thank you for helping me, Iosua," Theo said quietly. He wasn't sure what else to say. "How did you know about...me?"

"Your friend Cove was understandably worried about you. I offered to help."

"He did most everything. I only told him about you," Cove corrected. "And at that, I don't *recall* telling him, either. He saw you arrested, I think."

Theo smirked. It was so like Cove to correct a man that had helped her and him both.

"It is thanks to information that a man named Rune provided for me some months back when my cousin was imprisoned," Iosua said. "So if you see him around, you can thank him."

"I won't see him around, but I appreciate him," Theo said, only half-joking. He *was* thankful, and he *wouldn't* see this Rune. But at any rate, he had a good feeling about Iosua. The man radiated goodness and sunshine, something Theo hadn't felt in a long time; not since he was three or so. Before his father grew embittered against Theo and the prejudices his existence brought against the family.

Theo shook the thoughts aside. "Are you from the Red Quarter?" he asked Iosua.

"My family was exiled to the Red Quarter," Iosua said carefully. Cove's hand tightened on Theo's arm, as if she were listening intently too. Trying to figure something out. "But I suppose I don't ascribe to one Quarter or another."

"In the prison, people were calling for the removal of the king and his sons. Erik especially. There's a growing amount of unrest toward the Quarters being split, too," Theo said. He turned toward Cove. "Wouldn't that be something? Someday, we might be neighbors once again."

"You were neighbors at one point?" Iosua asked.

"Yes. Until his parents exiled him to the Black and abandoned him," Cove bit out.

Theo's stomach twisted with discontent at her anger. His parents had only done what they thought was best, and he missed the days when little Cove used to bring news of his family. Before she became too embittered against them. But he supposed she didn't owe him anything.

Not with what he knew and kept secret about her father. If she knew...well, that bitterness would be aimed earnestly, rightfully, and completely against him.

SEVEN

Cove

The next morning, Cove put on the nicest dress she owned—aside from the one for her betrothal party—and glanced down at the new stain deep in the flesh on her left arm. A permanent reminder of the murderous thoughts she'd held toward Erik the day before. It crept, tendrils reaching for her armpit. And then it would cross her clavicle and—

She hurriedly pulled her dress the rest of the way on, then ripped a brush through her thick brown curls. She darted out into the cramped kitchen and kissed her mother on the cheek. "I'll see you this evening. I have to speak with Erik."

Mother made a face, but nodded. "I worry about you, Cove. Don't do anything rash. You know how you are."

"I won't." She swallowed hard. "Well...I did yesterday, but I have to make it up to him now."

"Will he accept you back? He's an unruly man and...well, I wouldn't be surprised if you put one another into an early grave. Word spread fast that you stormed from the manor yesterday, and even more word spread that you were seen helping a boy from the Black Quarter. With another man. Cove, I will not have that feast of rumors coming from my home. I know it's just you, me, and Grandmother...but it still matters. We still have pride to uphold, and *you* your father's name. Though that barely matters anymore." Her voice caught, and Cove's heart twinged.

Rarely did Mother show remorse over losing her husband so young. Mostly, she was bitter. Angry. Hurt. But those instances of sincerity were coming more often now that Cove was set to leave soon, starting her own family, and losing her maiden name.

Cove Brandy. It had a ring to it that *mattered,* whether her mother appreciated it or not. She'd always warned Cove of being her father's daughter.

"I promise to make you proud," Cove said carefully. She wasn't sure how. Ever since Father's passing, Mother had been increasingly difficult to please. But wouldn't having a daughter with access to the Gold Quarter mean something?

She kissed Mother's cheek again and slipped out the back door, thankful to have avoided Grandmother for the time being. She would have harsher judgments and a harsher tongue still. She would presume Cove was involved with all three men, like as not. A shudder ran through her at the thought; imagining Iosua stooping to such a level felt disgusting, and she was already dreading such involvement with Erik. Theo...

Cove shut the door on her thoughts and kept her head bowed as she jogged toward the Quarter border, wishing again for a horse. It would allow faster transport. But Erik said she would have to marry him before having access to the nobility's stable.

It was the first thing that caught her attention with his engagement proposal.

Personal gain.

The notion hit her like a villager clipping her shoulder in passing, and her head whirled for a moment. Why did it matter? Of course it was advantageous, marrying the king's son, even though he was not the rightful heir. Of course it meant an obvious benefit to her and her family. Why else would she marry a man she barely knew? Why else, when she could barely tolerate him to begin with? Why else would she accept the verbal lashings, the slaps, the crude comments, the haughty looks?

Mother's words rang through her mind as she strode for Erik's manor, and each step brought a choppier gait and faster breath. What if she was right? Would Cove die from the curse by marrying him—and would she enrage him to the same extent? Why couldn't Cove just be happy? Most in their village would accept the privilege and not care about much else. Why couldn't she unpackage the beautiful gown he'd sent her, and twirl in it like a hapless little girl who just stepped into a fairytale come true?

Mind swirling, she nearly walked into the iron gate before she realized her feet must stop. Steadying herself, she nodded to the guard. "I am here to see Erik."

The guard nodded curtly. "He said to be expecting you. I won't say he's looking forward to this visit. You've sullied his family name. It might be wiser of you to turn around."

Hot embarrassment crept up her throat. And fear. But what else was she to do? Erik wouldn't help her. She had to do something for Theo. And Iosua just happened to be there to help!

Was it a crime to protect someone?

She stomped for his quarters, face hot and pounding with fear and anger, and found him with his nose buried in a book.

"Erik." She wanted to spit his name, to accuse him of spreading the rumors himself—because that's exactly what happened, after all—and to ask why he couldn't have just helped her himself. But all that came out was his name. He looked up, narrowing his eyes for a split moment. It was then she saw the black tendrils climbing up his neck.

The stains work their way up the neck, too? Not just into the heart? Cove wondered, confused. In her father, it had reached across his shoulder and dove straight for his heart. Same with all the other Red Quarters who died on the streets and laid naked, looted for their belongings before family could even find them. That's how the guards had found him. They had explained it in gruesome detail.

She swallowed hard. She'd branded Erik with this. Right? Or was he responsible for his own actions?

"Cove. You've created quite a rumor." He stood from his desk and rounded it, then leaned against the edge and crossed his arms, assessing her.

She stood at her full height and fingered the brooch clasping her cloak together at her neck; the only heirloom left from her father's family. "It wasn't by choice. I only helped someone. I am not responsible for what other people have said."

His lips twitched, but he spoke in a low, even tone that frightened Cove even more than screaming."Yesterday evening, my parents ordered me to the Citadel so we could discuss whether to turn you in to the guards or to pay the fee you incurred for breaking into the prison. The man you were with, and the prisoner? They didn't get their fees paid. So you can scurry off to the Black Quarter, or wherever you find scum like them, and tell them they're wanted men."

He tipped his chin up and stared down his nose.

Cove felt three inches tall when he looked at her that way.

She balled her hands into fists. She couldn't show the fear that struck her at the knowledge that both Theo and Iosua were in danger now. "So let them die. The curse, it will take them for their trespasses against king and kingdom. Same with me. That would make you happy, wouldn't it?" she threw back.

Erik lifted a brow. "I've chosen you, Cove. That decision is permanent. We sent out the town crier this morning to tamp down any rumors that might be had. And at any rate, the nobility in the Gold Quarter aren't exactly the most...loyal to spouses. You're simply getting an early start. I don't anticipate any problems with presuming whether or not a future child is my own, however. Is that correct?"

Cove's face burned hotter still with the accusation. "My people are more loyal than that! We marry for life. My own mother never remarried, never sought another man's arms after my father died. And I choose to live the same." It sickened her to have this peek behind the curtain in the nobility's lives. Did that mean he would seek pleasure with whomever his roving eye found? Of course she had known that going into this proposition. But why did it disgust her so? No rules spoke otherwise for the Gold Quarter. The Gold Quarter could choose any concubine they desired.

"Good. Because I need an heir, little sprite. For when the reign of King Lycidas is dismantled." The pet name turned her stomach. Erik moved forward, reached for her waist, and pulled her to him. "I told you of the vision I had where you wore the crown. My father may be king now, and my brother waiting in the wings, but if my plan comes to fruition? *You* will be my queen."

"The black on your neck. It's—from the argument, yes?" Cove braced her palms on his chest and pressed herself away enough to meet his dark eyes. She didn't want embraced by him. Never, truly. But especially not right now, while so many things swirled in her stomach like a cesspool. *My queen.* It screamed through her head.

"Yes. Don't fret on it. Have you tried on the gown?"

She blinked rapidly. He would be upset to hear her answer. "Well—Mother said something today about us putting each other into an early grave. I'm not going to do that to you, am I?"

He laughed. "Your mother is a simple person. Cove, there are rituals that can keep the curse satisfied. Blood sacrifice. A life in exchange for a life. The nobility does it all the time; it's only you people in the more rudimentary Quarters that reject such opportunities. The prisoners satisfy that need. Two problems, one incredibly efficient solution. The book I was studying, as a matter of fact, discusses those rituals. Care to join me in my studies?"

Cove wanted to vomit.

That's *truly* what they did with prisoners?

There had been rumors, certainly. But they were just that. Rumors, like Cove being involved with Theo and Iosua. The notion was absurd. But this one...it was confessed by a Gold Quarter's mouth like it was a simple fact of life. For him, it was.

Theo nearly paid for the debt of a man who could barely possess a tenth of Theo's own compassion and bravery. And if Theo or Iosua were caught...they would face that fate. Again.

Life for a life.

She pressed her lips together as Erik's mouth descended toward her. "No—I must get home. I simply wanted to smooth things over with you before..."

"This will help smooth things over," Erik said with a smirk. He tried again, and she pushed away harder.

"Erik. No. Before the betrothal party, even?" she scoffed, though it made her feel sick to be used in such a way.

She was not a righteous woman, nor did she know any personally. But this felt *wrong*. Her skin crawled.

She couldn't go through with this. Could she?

Iosua promised he knew a cure to the curse. One that would conquer it once and for all. That meant the blood sacrifices would no longer be necessary. Right?

A man like Iosua wouldn't even dream of acting like Erik. Even her father, as temperamental of a man as he was, never would have suggested such things to Cove. And Theo...he would be raging mad if he knew what Erik was suggesting. And rightfully so.

Was this the life she would choose?

Did she even have a choice now? She hadn't realized it until Iosua. She had hoped that this would be an escape, a change for the better. She would marry Erik, get the dowry for her mother and grandmother, and die the early death everyone anticipated for her. No, *this* was a living nightmare. Would Erik force her to participate in the blood sacrifices, too?

Erik's eyes darkened rapidly as he stared at her. "What is at home that is infinitely more important than me?"

"The...the dress. Of course, I need to try the dress on and get the measurements to your seamstress," she babbled. "I'm already late—"

He nodded, but his jaw ticked. In a flash, his hand was clenching her neck, his mouth against her ear as he hissed, "If I get word that you visited that sick, blind boy, I'll do as I please, Cove. And I think we both know what that will entail. I have guards watching you. Your family. Your friends. Or whoever they are."

He let her go, pushing her toward the door.

"I'll see you in time for the betrothal party. No earlier." His voice fell flat, emotionless.

Her chest rose and fell in heaves, and she forced herself to take measured steps until she reached the boundary into the Red Quarter, where her trembling body finally gave up and collapsed. On the cobblestone, she crouched on all fours and dry-heaved away the smell of his cologne.

She was being watched.

Controlled.

And the thought couldn't even make her angry right now.

No, it was much worse.

She was filled with terror.

And if she didn't help Iosua get the cure to the curse, she would be Erik's little heifer: a creature to produce his offspring as he pleased, and a sacrifice when he was not. That much was crystal clear, if not read between his words.

She was destined for death whether she served Erik or not. But her family and friends were under his threat, too.

And will he protect my family even if I do marry him? Will he keep his word? Cove thought. It weighed on her neck like a millstone, a new realization dawning that she could no longer look away from. A liar was a liar in all fronts of life...and Erik would be no different.

She had to go home and tell her mother and grandmother to be careful. And in the dark of night, she would disappear and find Iosua. If it was the last thing she did.

EIGHT

THEO

"THE INHABITANTS OF THE Red, Black, and Grey Quarters are hereby invited to a celebration of betrothal in the Citadel of the Gold Quarter. Prince Erik, son of Lycidas, and Red Quarter civilian Cove Brandy are announcing their blissful betrothal with a ball. You are expected to attend with proper dance attire, and the meal will be served at promptly six o'clock in the evening two weeks hence." The town crier split Theo's skull with his nasally, loud shout. Over and over again.

And it reverberated deep inside his chest.

Cove was betrothed?

To Erik?

He swallowed hard. Perhaps it was ridiculous of him to think Cove, the little girl from his childhood, could care a smidge about him. But he'd thought she was better than that. He'd always imagined getting out of the Black Quarter, revoking his curse somehow and fully seeing her for the first time in his life.

Even better if he could take her as his wife. Finally take care of her instead of the reverse always being true.

Now that privilege was given to a man as temperamental and rageful as Erik, the man who took pleasure in terrorizing the

Black Quarter, causing them to sin against him so they could be taken into prison.

Or simply imposing rules that nobody could realistically abide by.

Like the rule about the Black Quarter inhabitants being invited to the ball, but they had to wear proper dress attire. How could Solmere's beggars, the lame, blind, deaf, and mutes, find finery in exchange for a free meal? If they showed up in nothing but the best, they would be executed. If they didn't show up at all, they would be executed.

Just another way to torment the lowly living in the Quarters. Theo squeezed his eyes shut even though it wouldn't cast him into any deeper darkness.

His neighbor scuffed on the cobblestone as he shuffle-crawled closer. "Theo. You all right?"

"Yes. I just have a headache, it seems."

"It should be gone soon," the man said with a bit of a chuckle. "The town crier is leaving. Give him a few minutes and he'll be in the next block over, screaming the news. Isn't that the girl..."

"Yes." Theo cut him off curtly.

Silence met his ears, and he wondered if his neighbor had left him too. Perhaps he deserved it. It was his fate in life, it seemed.

"Who will you have, then? He won't let her out of the manor after they're wed. I guarantee it. She'll be..." His neighbor sucked in a sharp breath and said no more.

He didn't have to.

Theo heard all the rumors and knew what it would be for Cove.

But who was he to tell her she couldn't?

He was nothing. It stung to admit, but he knew it. Deep in his heart.

"Maybe that other man will help. Iosua, was it?" the neighbor asked. "I've heard rumors about him, too. Some say he'll overthrow the kingdom. Others that he's just a rabble-rouser. Some of the Black Quarter, the ones who can, go to listen to him sometimes. He teaches. I don't know what, though."

Theo shrugged one shoulder. "I don't even know where Cove found him, or if he's from this kingdom or simply a man passing through. Nobody knows. I certainly don't, and how would I find him again?"

"I could help you. Be your eyes."

"I'd have to carry you on my back."

"Good. Then we'll help each other." The neighbor laughed. "You're too scrawny, I think."

"Oh, whatever befalls us, befalls us. We've got one another for now. Right?"

The neighbor patted Theo's shoulder. "Yes. We do. Don't let the Gold Quarter convince you otherwise."

Until one or the other ended up arrested and thrown into prison. Again. Theo didn't voice this thought, but simply swallowed it. "Hey, if you climb up on my shoulders and we find a long gentleman's coat, d'ya think they'd let us into Erik's residence?" Theo asked instead. It was more amusing than planning the rest of his miserable life without...well, without her.

His neighbor laughed. "I suppose they'd take us straight to the Citadel's sacrifice altar at that point."

"Wouldn't even hide it, hm?" Theo mused. "Well, I'd be useless to help you in that case. The altar could bite me and I wouldn't even know it was there."

The neighbor chuckled. "Kind of like Cove, huh? Didn't even see it coming. *You*, I mean."

Theo shrugged one shoulder. "The nobles choose whomever they want in order to keep the peace between the quarters. Or to sate their own pleasure. Who am I compared to a nobleman, anyway? Perchance I'll find a lovely girl someday, here in the Black Quarter."

"Better look for a blind one, boy. You ain't too grand to look at." His neighbor snickered.

"Perfect pair. Thanks." Theo reached out to slap at the neighbor, but couldn't find him, only empty air. "That's a low blow."

"Do you need anything to eat, kid?" he asked, changing the subject again. "I got some extra from the market. Someone gave me some change."

"Gave, or...?"

"I'm offering you food. Don't ask where it came from."

That settled Theo's rumbling stomach. "I'm fine, thanks. I wasn't really hungry anyway."

"The headache?"

"What happened before the headache arrived," Theo corrected, since they were still speaking in riddles.

"Hm." The man sighed. "Well, this shall pass. You'll forget her. If she loves Erik, perhaps she wasn't the best woman herself."

Theo listened to the man drag himself away, but he wanted to argue. Say that Cove was worth far more than Erik would ever know, and she just couldn't see it. Tell the neighbor that he was all wrong. That maybe it wasn't her choice at all. Tell Cove, too, that she had choices. Options.

And he wanted to warn her that she was in a dangerous snare Theo never wanted to see closed around her throat.

He shook his head and settled against the stone wall nearby, listening for birdsong.

But there was none; only the soft tread of shoes passing through and the occasional scrape of a lame person passing.

He'd best get used to the gnawing pangs in his stomach, and the pain in his heart.

Maybe this meant the tendrils were growing closer to his heart, and he wouldn't have to endure the town crier announcing Cove's wedding. Their firstborn. The subsequent children. And her death.

Not Cove, the little girl who used to be his eyes.

Not the neighbor who didn't see him differently, until his parents kicked him out, convinced they could plead for a hearing and advance themselves to the Gray Quarter through good behavior—better odds at food, less prejudice—if they got rid of Theo. The little cursed boy.

Not Cove, the one who searched for him and brought him bread and nibbles of snacks and news from all over.

Not Cove, the girl he had to give up loving.

NINE

Cove

Cove pushed through the crowd, scouring every face she saw. Panic crept up her throat, which was sore from Erik's clenched grip. She hated that he had touched her. She hated that she'd *let* him. And she hated imagining that more would come. Her father would have murdered Erik for what he'd done—no, simply for what he'd suggested. Father had been a proud man, and a violent one to be certain; and that had brought about his own death. But so was Erik, tenfold.

Erik was a handsome face hiding all the darkness in the world. And all the bitterness in Cove's own veins couldn't begin to amount to the sins coursing through his own hard heart. Something wicked propelled him forward in life, she was sure of it. She could sense it thrumming beneath his skin, a force beyond her own.

Just like she'd sensed with Iosua. Only the opposite. Something deep inside her had cringed away from him, but she knew she was safe. She knew he was safe.

And right now, she needed him.

She pushed through the southeasternmost corner of the Red Quarter and into the Black. If she'd met him there, surely he would be there again today. Right? She'd never seen him in the Red. And she couldn't venture into the Gray Quarter. The guards were more vigilant there than they were in the Black. And why wouldn't they be? There were better people to watch over there. More money. Less filth. Longer-living families than the Red or the Black.

Which was certainly why Erik had chosen her...wasn't it? A girl from the Red Quarter who would give him what he wanted with little need for loyalty. Use her, abuse her, and search for a new willing participant before she was even spent.

She should have listened to Mother when she had encouraged her to hide the day his servants came knocking at the door.

Too late now.

Shoving her way through the crowd, she heard a town crier shouting the merry news.

She was getting married.

And everyone was invited to the betrothal ball.

She muttered dark things against Erik. "He's doing this so I can't get away."

But she'd prove him otherwise.

And she'd find this cure for herself, and for Theo, before Erik could hurt anyone else. Before he could use anyone else for his own spiteful gain.

She raced through the alley Theo usually lived in, casting a *hush yourself* look toward his neighbor. She would see Theo later, but she couldn't stop right now. She would be back for him when she had a cure.

"You're not from the Black, but I'd wager you're Red. Let me guess: are you the betrothed? I heard the news." A voice appeared next to her ear, and she muffled a shriek with her hands, spinning on her heel and coming face-to-face with a strange man. He snatched her arm in a tight grip before she could bolt, but he didn't do so harmfully. Just firm. She drew back her free fist to crunch his nose and he held up his other hand defensively. "I know Iosua. He told me to keep an eye out for you."

She stilled. "And you are?"

"Rune."

She sucked in a deep breath and forced herself to relax. "I've heard of you."

He nodded. "You gonna listen, or do I have to hold you still?"

"I'll listen. Please."

The man nodded, his sharp, dark eyes glancing quickly over her before letting go. "Seems you've been held against your will already." He nodded toward her neck.

She shifted her cloak, though it wouldn't cover the red marks. "Is Iosua here?"

"He had to leave on a journey, but he wants us to catch up with him a few days hence. Are you going to help?"

"He promised there was a cure for...for this curse." Cove rolled up her sleeves, baring her stained forearms. Tears welled up over her cheeks as she noticed how black her fingertips were now, after fleeing Erik.

"Yes. Are you willing to follow Iosua?"

"Maybe. Where is it?" Cove asked. "The cure?"

"That is information only Iosua knows," Rune said. "Did he tell you who I am?"

"A follower?"

Rune sighed impatiently. "Yes, but also a zealot for the Order of Gray Exiles. We are a group of men from the Gray Quarter who seek to overturn the Gold Quarter and restore freedom to the other regions of Solmere."

A chill swept over Cove. There were rebels working in silence? For how long? "Is Iosua going to start a riot? Overturn the kingdom?"

"I believe so," Rune said. "Which is why he is so secretive. But it comes at a cost for everyone involved. There's something planned for the same day the Citadel is celebrating your betrothal. The same day followers of Iosua will celebrate the feast of the slain lamb. News has been spreading faster than the town crier can share, since we have informants on our side. Like me."

She stilled. "You're a guard too?"

"*Former.*" He bit the words out so sharply she took a step back.

"I understand."

"This journey will come at a cost, and you should know that. If it fails, we won't be able to return here to live. It could mean death. It could mean fleeing Solmere. It could mean your family, if you have one, is captured and killed. And even if it's successful, it will come at a steep cost for some."

Rune's eyes bore into hers, but she swallowed hard, standing tall.

"You expect this to be fearsome for me? My fate is already death. I'd rather have it be for something honorable than...the alternative."

He quirked a brow. "Erik."

"Yes. But why the Citadel? How will overthrowing the Citadel reverse the curse?"

"Iosua believes there is a cure. There is a prophecy of a sharp, stone crown, and another one called Life—I can't recall what exactly it says, but whoever conquers shadow will wear it. King Lycidas *can't*."

"Why not?" Cove asked.

"Because." Rune gestured her forward, and she found a tiny hut up against the back of the bakery wall. It was scattered with various daggers, leather armor, and not much else. She shivered in the cold. At least she had a home to go to.

"We can talk here, quietly, without the eyes of the guards," Rune explained. "King Lycidas may wear a physical crown, but he cannot wear the one given to the conqueror of shadow. To do so would necessitate casting out the darkness he relies on. The curse runs deep, Cove, but it's reversible. You'll learn more later, as you are ready. But there are powers at work in the world. The king and all of his men, all of the nobility, and many of the Gray Quarter have fallen asleep, lulled there by the curse itself. And yes, they continue to feed it by blood sacrifice." Rune trailed off, a troubled expression furrowing his brow. "Iosua has kept the details secret, of what must occur to cast the shadow into the depths."

"Can we trust him?" Cove asked. "Would he lead us to the crown? What if we used Erik? Even if it meant tricking him..." Cove trailed off, contemplating her next words. The weight they held. Was it worthwhile? "If it meant protecting my family and Theo and everyone I care about, I would let Erik do as he saw fit to me. Perhaps that could be in exchange—"

Rune held up a hand. "No, Cove. We will not win by deceit, nor by accepting the curse as our own and furthering its roots within us. But Iosua said he wants your help. And there are a few others that I have made arrangements with already, people who will join us. It's a dangerous journey and an even more perilous battle to win, to be conqueror."

Cove took in a shuddering breath. "Would it protect my family, at least? If Theo's in danger..."

Rune tipped his head, thinking. "I can't promise that. But if we are successful, the curse will be shed by anyone who chooses to accept the Conqueror and not the curse."

Cove gave a slight, barking laugh. "Nobody I know would choose the curse over a cure."

Rune raised a brow. "You have much to learn. But that can be done on the road. And you will want Theo with us, partly to protect him from the forces that will otherwise descend on him in our absence, and also because he is necessary. Incredibly so."

Cove swallowed hard. "Can I have a few days to think about it?"

Rune's lips twitched impatiently, but he nodded. "I'll find you when it's time."

TEN

Cove

"Look for me and you will find me," Cove murmured over and over. She burst from her cottage door and hung a sharp left away from the village that promised so much trouble. She needed time alone, time to breathe. Time to sort out the angry tensions in her heart. The last thing she wanted was to watch her veins darken black against her mother or her grandmother's words. To prove that she was no better than her father who died before her.

The one who sealed the curse she would suffer from, too.

Theo's own mother, the one who had abandoned him to the Black Quarter, had swung by the morning prior to let them know she'd seen Cove dipping into a hut with another man—Rune—but nobody else knew that. Cove had argued that the woman had been disobeying rules herself, visiting the Black Quarter for bread when she couldn't be bothered to visit one alleyway down and see her own son. But that had only brought out more vicious dressing-downs from Mother, who grabbed Cove's shoulders and shook her until her teeth rattled.

"Don't you know what's good for you?" Mother had snapped. "Erik and his money will help all of us! You made your choice, now keep it. If you keep going..."

She'd trailed off, eyed the fingerprints around Cove's neck, and then suddenly let go of her.

"Go somewhere. I don't want to see you today," she'd said, turning away.

"They're from Erik," Cove said, taunting. "These marks. He's not your savior, and he's not mine either!"

But Mother had turned away, back to her mending basket. Grandmother stared at the wall. Deaf to Cove's words. Of course she was. So Cove decided she couldn't stand being near them either, and bolted out the door.

Her family would despise her for marrying Erik, and they would despise her for not taking advantage of the privilege if she figured out how to escape or break free from her promise. Not to mention, it wasn't necessarily a choice she had a say in. A villager could not deny a nobleman's proposal of marriage. Not without punishment, anyway, and she had nothing to lose but her life...and even that was approaching dusk.

"Look for me, and you will find me, huh? *How*?" She stormed into the woods, through twisted brambles that caught her stockings and her boots, even ripping her skirts. She couldn't afford to replace such clothes. Not without marrying Erik. And then, what would the point be? He would suck the life from her and be on to the next, she was quite sure.

After this week, she couldn't bear the thought of him. She clenched her teeth and her fists.

Her own bitterness would kill her if he didn't.

And there was Iosua promising help. Promising an escape. A man who knew far too much than he should. How? Maybe it was a trap after all. It wouldn't surprise her. But she didn't sense it, couldn't smell deceit on him...not like she could with Erik at first. She reacted viscerally to Iosua, to be sure, but it was an overt awareness of being too...*wrong* to be near him. Too full of darkness, bitterness, hatred. He exposed the bad parts and made her wish they weren't so blatant. She could tolerate such feelings as long as her people were safe.

Theo. And even if they didn't want it right now, Mother and Grandmother.

Yes. If her world was safe, she would be happy, no matter what it took.

"Look for me, and you will find me. How can I follow someone who does not appear when he ought to?" Cove asked, stopping in a clearing. She stooped, hands on knees, to catch her breath. At least she could breathe out of sight from Erik. None of his men would deign to enter this forest. Too difficult.

How often would she get out here if she wed Erik? It was her favorite haunt; another connection she had to her father. He'd spent days on end treading the forest, hunting stags, gathering edible plants and berries and mushrooms. He often bailed outside when Mother became overbearing.

"You're just like him, you know. Always slipping out to that forest, that twisted little deer-path that he loved so much." Mother would tell her in softer, gentler moments of her youth. Brushing away her matted brown curls, Mother would plant a kiss on Cove's smooth brow and whisper stories of gentler times, when Father was still alive and not consumed in his own thoughts. Now, it was a taunt; a grim reminder that Cove had a temper to match her father as well.

"Are you searching for Iosua?"

The familiar voice caught Cove's breath from her very lungs, and she straightened, spinning to face him.

"Rune. How did you find me?"

"Don't speak my name so loudly," he chided. He was on foot, wearing worn leather armor and a sword at his side. "I was assigned to search for a man in the Red Quarter. Now you must answer *my* question."

"How do you know Iosua? You didn't tell me earlier," she answered instead.

Rune sucked in a breath that suggested he had better things to do than entertain her suspicions. "I've heard of him. Watched him for a time, until I decided he was worth listening to. He offered the same to me."

Cove's face contorted in frustration. "He was just here a few days ago, and..." Should she admit to that? Or would it put Theo in danger somehow?

Rune wouldn't turn her in. Surely not, given his disdain toward the guards and nobility. Still, it couldn't hurt to keep the confession shut up. She lifted her chin. "Well, that is, I was searching for him and have yet to find him."

"Funny thing about men like Iosua. They won't be found, but they will find you when you least expect."

"And what kind of man is Iosua?" she asked, tipping her head. "Unless you have better places to be."

Rune shifted his weight from one foot to another, clearly impatient. "A man with purpose. Vision. Clarity as I have never seen before. I do have elsewhere to attend. But make no mistake, the first moment I find Iosua again, I will abandon this sword and I will follow him. I believe he intends to overthrow the governing forces. And I believe he will do abundantly more than anyone in my sect could possibly hope to achieve. Have you made your decision?"

"Well, Rune, I would love to. But it seems we must find this man first," Cove said sarcastically, swinging her arms wide.

He chuckled, shaking his head. "I've heard rumor that he is heading for the Gray Quarter. If that is true, you and I will not find him until he *wants* to be found. You know the laws. He has to be careful. Just like we do."

"I thought you disdained the laws," Cove pointed out. "And I'm fairly immune to fearing them, too."

Rune smirked, something flashing in his dark eyes. "Well, that's a clever way of putting it. What do you propose, then?"

Before, she'd been uncertain. Nearly sick with the decision before her. But after being met with such vitriol by her own home, resolve flooded her. She would take Theo. Her mother and grandmother would be safer far away from her. And it would free her up to do whatever must be done to seek the strange cure that Iosua rambled on about.

What had she to live for if all else was stripped from her grasp? Why wouldn't she try to make a change, do what no one else was brave enough to do, and change her bloodline before she fell to the same fate everyone expected of her?

"I say we leave soon. Go in search of him in the Gray Quarter. What do we have to lose but our lives? We'll lose them if we stay, surely. At least I will, and I'm sure your line of work isn't…necessarily approved by Erik or those above him."

Rune took a deep breath, staring at her with wide eyes that betrayed his surprise. Cove felt a wriggle of amusement that she'd shocked this zealot. "You're serious."

"Yes, quite."

He laughed, a cawing sort of sound that startled both Cove and a few birds in the tree branches above. "I like your spirit, girl. Tomorrow night, meet me on the boundary between the Red and the Black Quarter."

"I'll already be there."

"Why?"

"Theo. He'll want to come too."

"You talked it over with him?"

"No."

Rune again chuckled, brows raised. "Very well. We'll need all the men we can get."

"He's blind, completely," Cove added.

Rune paused, a grimace crossing his face. "Truly? I thought it was only hearsay from the guards."

"Yes. And I will not hear anything of leaving him behind. I must protect him."

He stared at her, steady and firm, and Cove stared right back. "He has heightened senses in hearing and perception. He will be helpful."

Rune shook his head with a dry laugh. "We're dooming ourselves from the beginning. Fine. Tomorrow night."

ELEVEN

Cove

After Cove returned to her house that night, neither her mother nor her grandmother looked at her. Their arms now sported fresh, black veins at their elbows. Identical. Perhaps they had the same temper, which ran long then snapped violently after too much pressure. And here Cove was, the temperamental one who took after the man her mother could neither let go nor forgive.

Their silence ran into the next morning, when Mother simply looked at Cove and shook her head. "You cannot back out from the betrothal now, Cove. You'll be killed either way. I can't believe you."

A million angry retorts flew to the forefront of Cove's mind, but she bit each one back with effort, shoveling her lumpy oat mash into her mouth. Either she'd remain silent or she'd choke on breakfast. And then where would her family be?

Still, her chest burned each time she saw the fresh stains on her mother's arms. Grandmother had yet to rouse, but her anger would be even more intolerable. Suddenly, tears smarted behind her eyes. It was *her* fault they were so angry. All of it was her fault. She'd acted out of turn. She'd been belligerent. She'd been insulting. She'd acted without regard to society. And her mother would pay the price.

It was her choice to get so angry, Cove thought. But no—it was Cove's choice just as much as it was Mother's.

"Well? Aren't you going to say anything to that?" Mother asked after several long, tense moments passed in silence.

Cove's spoon clinked against the bowl once, twice, three times as she scraped up the last of her breakfast.

"No," she finally said at length. Rising from her chair, she added, "Sell the garments that arrived. There will be no need for the dress, but there will be a need for food soon."

Mother's eyes bulged and her face turned scarlet. "Cove!" Mother slammed her own bowl onto the table and set hands on hips archly.

"I have a plan. But I cannot tell you more about it. You wouldn't be safe if I did."

She shook her head, scoffing. "Running away, just like your father used to."

Cove's ire rose and she clenched her teeth. "Yes. Just like Father. You always tell me that, so why not make everyone proud in their assumptions?" she asked angrily. Heat flared up her arms and she sucked in a sharp breath. The stains near her shoulders were burning. She had to stop.

"Now—" Mother's face softened, but Cove darted from the table to her room, where she locked herself in. Mother and Grandmother shared the room next to hers, and she could hear Grandmother snoring loudly through the thin wall as she packed her spare dress, snappily tied her boot laces tight, and fastened her family's cloak and heirloom brooch and cloak keeper to her breast. It was a small, gray woolen cloak that wouldn't serve well to keep anyone warm, but it was part of her. It was given it to her on her fifth birthday, passed down from Mother's sister who died very young, and Father insisted on giving it to Cove early. At five, Cove swam in its size. But now, it fit across the shoulders perfectly and fell down to her knees. And the brooch, a bloodred ruby fixed inside an intricate metal flower, the last remnant of her father's family. It was one she would bear with pride. It was one she would bear with honor, if she made it as far as finding the cure Iosua and Rune spoke of. And she would die with it fixed to her cloak, no matter how the end would meet her.

"Theo, it's Cove. You need to wake up," Cove whispered, gently shaking Theo's shoulder as he slept slumped against the bakery wall. The stones radiated the night's cold dampness, and she shuddered. To sleep here, always and forever, was a misery she hated for her friend. And if fate had it, she would make sure he never did again.

He jerked awake, and she clapped a hand over his mouth. "Don't say anything. It's me, Cove."

His breathing, once a frantic staccato, leveled out and he finally nodded. She let go of his mouth.

"Why—what're you—what's wrong, Cove?" he asked finally.

"I'm going with a man, Rune, to find the cure. To find Iosua, the man who helped you. And I want you to come with me, because I can't help you if I'm gone."

Theo's face was barely visible in the weak moonlight, but she still made out a frown. "Cove, are you sure? It's not safe to—"

"If you wish to stay, you can. But I fear for your life. Something Iosua said before. And I want to get you out of here, but I can only do that if you go willingly. I want to fix this."

"Fix *what*?" Theo stared over her left shoulder, so Cove could easily avoid the worry in his eyes, but frustration radiated off of him nonetheless.

"The curse. I want to find the cure, and I want to change everything about the way we live. I don't want to fear trespassing through the Quarters anymore. I don't want to fear Erik or the king and his men anymore. I don't want to live in a world that says *you* are wicked and broken. I don't want to live in a world that demands I die for who I am," she blurted. All at once, the weight of the mission ahead of her rested on her shoulders. "I don't know how much I can achieve now, but I want to do something."

"Help me up," Theo said. "Who's Rune, again?"

"I'm going to meet him at the border of the Red Quarter at the quarter of the hour. I don't have much time, Theo. Is this goodbye?"

Her friend put an arm around her shoulders, and her heart plummeted. Of course, he wouldn't come with her. It was foolish to believe otherwise—

His embrace crushed her close. "I know you'll make a difference, and I know the nobles will tremble to see you coming. Let's go."

THE PROPHECY

TWELVE

Theo

"So you're the boy who escaped Erik," the strange man addressed Theo.

Theo thrust a hand forward and was met with open air instead of a hand to shake. He waited a few beats, then let it drop to his side. *Off to a stellar start.* Cove's hand tightened around his arm.

"Iosua and I saved him from prison," Cove supplied. "But he didn't do anything wrong."

"The imprisoned rarely do," the stranger said. "That's how the nobility operates. Learn that now, and learn it quick. If you haven't already."

"I have," Cove argued.

"To a point," Theo added quietly. He hadn't explained his experience in the jail to Cove yet. Something was brewing. Something big and ugly. The town crier's announcement still rattled painfully through his mind. Was Cove using this man to get away from Erik? Or was she pretending to pledge fealty to this man? *Rune*, he reminded himself. Names weren't his strong suit. Since he couldn't see faces to remember anyone by, he resorted to recalling tonal qualities and hoping for the best.

Rune's voice was deep, gravelly, with a hint of derision that dripped in certain moments—like now.

"Yes, I agree with this one." A rough hand clapped on Theo's shoulder and he jumped. "Cove, you think you know the darkness, but you haven't seen it yet. Do you know what they were going to use Theo for?"

"No," Cove supplied.

"I do," Theo said. He stumbled over a log and Cove muttered an apology. "It's all well," he reassured her.

"What were they going to do?" Rune pressed.

"They were going to use me as a sacrifice of some sort. For Erik."

"Who are *they*?" Rune asked.

"I don't know. Guards." Theo shrugged. What did the man expect of him?

"See, you know not what you are up against. The guards and Erik are beholden to the king. The king is beholden to another man above him. A counsellor of some sort. And there is a master. Someone they fear most passionately. Erik has pledged fealty to him, and is rising in the ranks rapidly. They take the most innocent people from the streets and sacrifice them to this master. The master prolongs the life in their stone hearts, lest they perish. He is known as The Deceiver." A long pause followed. "Cove, it appears you could have benefitted from such arrangements."

Fabric rustled and Theo wondered if she was tightly covering up her arms with her cloak. Her hand left his arm for a moment before finding its way back, squeezing tight. "You don't know that. I would never accept such *help*. And especially not from Theo's...death."

"So it does not surprise you, their evil plots?" Rune asked. "They intend to slowly cull off anyone who is not beneficial to their nation. At first, it was the elderly. Then, the disabled. Now it is anyone who crosses the Quarters. Anyone who disobeys. Anyone who disagrees with Erik."

Another uncomfortable silence blankets us. "That includes you," Theo said quietly to Cove, in the general direction of her ear. Her frizzy hair brushed against his nose.

"I know. But that's why we're doing what we are doing, yes, Theo? We must stop their plans before it comes down to murdering one another."

"It will take murder to reach them," Rune mused. Theo heard the bristly sound of Rune rubbing a hand over rough, short stubble. "Are you prepared?"

"Yes," Cove answered confidently. Theo only hoped she did not come to the point of murdering someone; she didn't know the pain it would inflict. Theo had never killed another, but he'd heard and experienced many die. Tried to comfort some. And it only led to grief upon grief. Especially...

No. Not right now. He shoved the thought aside. He couldn't imagine how difficult it would be for those gifted with sight to viscerally watch the end descend upon someone.

"We'll find Iosua. But we need to find a few friends of ours first," Rune said, sparking Theo's attention back to the present.

He listed off three people: Bo, a wise old man and a priest. Arne, a steadfast man that sounded like their best option for overtaking the king's reign even if the prophesied cure was not found. And there was Ingrid, Arne's wife.

Theo wordlessly listened on as Cove argued ardently against gathering more people, and Rune guided them through thick foliage, warning them of briars and low-hanging branches he pulled back for them. He ignored Cove entirely and insisted his way was better; he was more informed, more involved, and more prepared. And though Theo couldn't yet put a finger on the pulse of who Rune was as a person, he had to admit that he and Rune agreed on one thing: they wouldn't let Cove get hurt, even if it meant enduring her anger. And the more people to protect her, the better.

THIRTEEN

COVE

"YOU KNOW HOW THE system works, right?" Rune asked as they walked through the cover of night. He'd been silently brooding for so long that Cove had begun scheming how to slip away and seek out the cure with Theo, abandoning Rune in his own thoughts. But now, he chose to speak. She stifled a huff of frustration.

"Sure. Iosua said a few things. About how...they wanted to kill Theo."

"But do you really understand the implications?" Rune asked. "Sure, we talk about the killings. But do you understand what it is for?"

Cove rolled her eyes. "Erik explained it to me. But clearly only *you* know the *truth* behind the matter."

She was pretty certain a taunting smirk was plastered on his face, and she was deciding whether to entertain wiping it off for him when he responded. "They were going to use him as a human sacrifice. That's what they do with all the innocents they kill. It's not just some magical mess where an innocent's good deeds are used to reverse the evil ones' misdeeds. There's an altar, a twisted ritual. *Not* a swift demise."

Theo's footsteps faltered. Cove reached for him as his hand slid off her arm, and she set it back up on her shoulder. "Are you well?" she asked.

"Y-yes." But the tremor in his voice spoke otherwise. "How would I be a suitable sacrifice? Don't the deities the men worship...don't they believe that only good sacrifices should be given up? I'm from the Black Quarter. I'm not...pure."

What would it take for Theo to realize he was kinder and more decent than most Cove knew? To push past the lie his parents seeded his mind with...when would that harvest cease? What if even this journey would not cure him? Would life without sight be good enough for Theo?

Rune cleared his throat loudly. "Yes, you're blind. But you..." He trailed off. "Your arms."

"I can't see them," Theo pointed out. "But if I'm a blemish to our kingdom, wouldn't their master see me as an improper sacrifice?"

"I understand where you're coming from, Theo. But that's assuming King Lycidas fully believes that you *are* blemished. It's proof that he knows what he is doing is perverse. And for your arms..." He paused for a few moments, the only sounds their boots treading over dry grass. Finally, he said, "You are less...offensive, less sinful than most."

Cove's brows furrowed. Why wouldn't he just tell Theo that he didn't have any black on his arms? Only a few stains on his fingertips. Before she could do the same, he plowed ahead.

"The Gold Quarter takes all its prisoners—there are prisons in the Red, Black, and Gray Quarters, yes?"

"We're not supposed to travel outside our respective Quarters, how would we know?" Cove asked, too sweetly.

"And yet, you're traveling with Theo," Rune shot back.

Cove snorted. "He was Red before he was exiled."

He chuckled. "At any rate. They imprison people for the slightest of infringements and some are transported to the Gray Quarter, exploit them, and sacrifice them. The blood sates their deities and they are granted longer lifespans. Do you know how many people truly die from those black stains, or do they die from the *executions*?"

Cove's heart burned with his question. Was he suggesting the curse wasn't real? Because it was all too real, and her life had been a misery for it. Anger welled up in her chest and she sucked in a deep breath to argue.

"We all know people who have died from the curse of the stone heart," Theo filled in quickly, speaking up before Cove could. She felt the knot in her stomach unfurl. "But if King Lycidas' deities can heal or prolong life...why can't that be made available to all of us? Who can reverse the curse? Without bloodshed?"

"There's a prophecy. Iosua spoke of it, something to put the end to all other deities, something to put to death the blood sacrifices, and the person to do so would wear the crown of Life. I don't know much—"

"He told me some of the same," Cove cut in. "But we need to find out what the prophecy is about. And follow through with it."

Rune held back a long branch and ushered Cove and Theo through ahead of him. As he let it snap back behind them, he said, "Don't you want to know more about the Gold Quarter?"

"How do you know so much?" Cove finally asked. Sure, he was a guard and a traitor to the king...but he had knowledge of their *deepest* secrets. Surely King Lycidas was not so foolish as to broadcast every little thing to his entire guard. Theo's grip tightened on her shoulder, a warning. But it was her job to protect them both.

Rune scoffed. "How don't you know this? I am part of a zealot group. They have been working for decades to overturn the Gold Quarter and return power to our people. We know things, we have traitors in high places. The Gold Quarter would have Iosua and anyone who believes him executed, you know."

"So the zealots have insiders with knowledge from the Gold Quarter?" Cove asked, hope springing in her chest. It thrummed through her veins, a fire that would not be squelched. Her father had railed against the nobles endlessly. Would *she* see an end to the reign he despised so much?

"Yes."

"There are rebels?" she asked. It hardly seemed possible. Her family had lived in Solmere for as long as she knew; perhaps they had always lived there from their first ancestors. And all had died under severe men, rulers with deeper appreciation for the darkness, severe punishments, and strange fetishes. Was this the end of an era?

Would she live to see it?

Theo squeezed her shoulder as if to confirm what she'd been thinking.

This strange thing, hope, was an impossible thing to destroy. And one day, perhaps, Theo would have a better life. Free from his curse. Free from the punishment of society, the hatred of his family. Her mother and grandmother could live free from the brand of knowing the one who died so young, so prideful, so angry. Maybe she would even get to see the end result, if she was careful. If she didn't perish on the way. If she didn't have to sacrifice herself—but she considered it impossible to satisfy a curse that thrived on bloodshed without more of the same. And even if she did die...

She would make them proud, even if she never got to see their joy.

FOURTEEN

Theo

His legs shook from exertion, but he forced them to keep moving. Even after Rune's revelation that there were people through all of the quarters seeking to overturn the Gold Quarter, his mind gnawed over the fact that he'd nearly been sacrificed to the dark world. Whatever it was. His family had never been followers of Solmere's deities, and as far as he was concerned, they were ahead for it. All of the deities seemed tempestuous, angry, bitter. Much like the people who died in Solmere for the same hardheartedness. Like Cove believed of her father.

But Mr. Brandy had never been truly evil like King Lycidas and his family. He'd been short-tempered, and Theo had sympathized with Cove for that fact. There were many nights Cove had spoken of when her father had been caught up in screaming matches with her mother. At one point, Theo imagined they had been in a happy union, and he was sorry it had devolved—especially that Cove only knew the bad parts. But Theo also knew something that Cove could never know, because he wasn't a valid eyewitness...which also meant he was never able to tell anyone who would listen.

Mr. Brandy had not died from the curse of the stone heart at all. He had been dropping off soup for Theo when the guards found him. He'd spat on the guards' boots and cursed them out for demanding him to leave. And Theo had felt the hot, sticky spray of blood across his face when her father was run through with a sword.

"Check his arms."

"They're black. Almost to his breastbone."

"Of course." The man spat, and Theo flinched as he imagined the spittle landing on Mr. Brandy. "Well, notify the family. Get the healer to clean and stitch up his wounds, dress him, before you deliver him to the family for burial. Say he dropped dead. They won't investigate further."

"Yes, sir."

Theo could never forgive himself for knowing, bearing witness, and most of all being the cause of Cove's father's death. The man had been cruel to an extent common to the Red Quarter; Cove had described violent outbursts, and when he and Cove lived near one another in their childhood, he could hear the man ranting against the Gold Quarter, screaming at his wife, and slamming doors.

Suddenly, he wondered if Mr. Brandy had known the man Theo heard in the prison days ago.

Cove's anger was not the violent type like her father before her. It was the type that turned inward, self-destructive. And why wouldn't it be? Her family, her whole world, told her she would wind up perishing foolishly like her father...and the entire story, as she knew it, was a farce to begin with.

And *now* Theo understood why they had checked the man's arms. Seeing someone delivering food to the sick Black Quarter would have implied that the man had a better, purer heart than most. Now, Theo could bet the guards would have rather taken the man as a sacrifice for the king. For his dukes, his masters, and whatever perverse idols he served. For Erik. Discomfort crawled up his arms, his stomach, his toes. He'd nearly become a sacrifice too. Nearly died for someone so wicked. If he died—no, *when*—he wanted it to be protecting someone worth loving. Someone worth more than she could ever see in herself...Sometimes, he was convinced she was blinder than him! But not just someone. It could only ever be Cove.

FIFTEEN

Cove

THEY FINALLY STOPPED AND slept for a short time before the sun's rising drove them deep into the woods to avoid being seen. It was then that Rune presented more of his plan, and Cove had her fingers crossed that he would give up the notion of bringing more people into this mission. While toppling King Lycidas' regime would save Solmere, the void would only create space for someone even darker to take the throne. Right? She didn't want to waste time on something like that. But she needed the cure. If she were to make an impact, it was going to be finding that cure and saving the people she loved.

If only Rune would shut up and see that.

"By evening, we'll reach the Gray Quarter. There's a pub I need to visit. There are two young people that work there that I think will be crucial to our mission. Arne and Ingrid."

Cove wrinkled her nose. *This again.* "Why bring more people into our mission? We have enough with just you, me, and Theo. More people will draw attention. I say we go for the cure and let the rest lie. There are enough rebels, from the sounds of it. And they have their own plan. Let them handle their portion. I only want the cure."

"You are not wrong in that more people will bring more attention," Rune said slowly, carefully. "But you are also *completely* wrong."

"Thank you. That's a stellar explanation and you have changed my mind unequivocally." Cove kicked a rock lying nearby.

Theo snorted at Cove's sarcasm and she smirked, glancing backwards at him. His face always scrunched up with boy-like joy when he laughed. And since he was blind, she couldn't fear him catching her gaze. She wasn't sure how he could be so pure and childlike when so much had happened to him. Perhaps if she understood, she could be more like him and stop worrying her mother to the point of hatred.

Only fear could breed such vitriol between mother and daughter.

"We need Arne and Ingrid because they are part of the Exiles, plus Bo," Rune explained. "The group is adjacent to the zealots; ardent followers of one called El Elyon. They will be sympathetic to our cause."

"Do they know Iosua?" Cove asked finally. If they were, maybe they could lead her to Iosua. And then she and Theo could split from Rune.

Rune studied her a moment. "Yes. I met Arne and Ingrid when they were following Iosua from the Gray Quarter to the Red. They are recognized as rebels because they defied the marriage laws. After their spouses died, they didn't turn to the king to request matches beneficial to society."

Cove wrinkled her nose. "Stupid system, anyway."

"Yes." Rune yanked a fallen branch off the path and kept walking. "Which is why I believe they will be an excellent addition to our team. They have experience flying under the radar. They want this change as more as anyone does. Even you, Cove." Rune paused. "They're good people," he added, softer this time.

"I believe you," Cove started. "But you even admitted that it was a good idea to stay in a smaller group, or—"

Rune waved her off with an impatient huff. "It's fine. Really. Arne is talented with swords, even if he does not admit it. Ingrid is a little easier to discount, but she is still critical to the mission. You'll understand when you see her. They're a package deal. Never been apart from each other."

Cove nodded slowly, not willing to appear agreeable. "How far away is the pub?"

Rune sighed with practiced patience. "A day's journey. We will reach the pub tonight, and hopefully Arne and Ingrid will give us a safe place to rest. We should be to the Gold Quarter's border within a few days, anyway. What is another day added onto that? Do you wish to die faster?"

Cove pressed her lips together. *You're a miserable, juvenile rat, Rune*, she retorted mentally. "It's fine," she said curtly. "But what of Bo? Don't expect me to heed any further delays."

"I would *never*, your highness," he said, downright taunting. Cove forced her feet to move forward instead of arguing further, cloak swishing with her rapid movements. She fingered the brooch holding the cloak shut at her throat. If she died, would someone be there to send the heirloom back to her mother? Would her mother accept it back, or simply discard it? Sell it? She supposed it wasn't hers to worry about.

If Rune only got out of the blasted way.

She only hoped it would be worthwhile.

SIXTEEN

Cove

The barrier between the Black and Gray Quarters was distinct. Sharp. Anyone who crossed the border accidentally would either be blind or lying. And, given the number of blind in the Black Quarter, it was likely the guards used that theory to arrest and imprison an untoward number of stricken people unfairly.

Tall stone structures loomed overhead, with very little cover by way of the forest. The streetways were mazes Cove couldn't see through. A bird's-eye view was the only thing that would possibly show them the route through—unless, of course, one was Rune and inexplicably knew every possible street, alley-way, and shortcut. He never slowed down even a moment, and Cove struggled to keep up and keep Theo from tripping.

The air wasn't putrid with rotting flesh, death, and human misery like the Black Quarter, but it held a certain chemical stench that made Cove's stomach churn. She almost pitied the people here, until she remembered that they would have her killed for setting foot in their Quarter. They distributed products, textiles, and special, buttery-smooth cloth for the Gold Quarter and exported it worldwide, while their neighbors in the

Black and Red Quarters struggled to eke out enough produce to survive through harsh winter, recycling worn-out cloth to be a pitiful semblance of 'new.' Cove had never felt a brand-new piece of cloth in her life, she realized. Her face flushed hot. How harshly would Arne and Ingrid judge her? And what about poor Theo?

"Do we need these people?" she asked Rune sharply. Only after she'd said it did she realize he wouldn't have a clue why she was so abrupt. She'd hardly spoken since Rune's acrid comments earlier.

He turned a cross glance toward her. "Arne and Ingrid? Yes. We do. They will know where Iosua is. We already went over this."

"I don't think any follower of Iosua could be *here*," she snapped, sticking her nose in the air only to choke on thick smoke that was nothing like the woodsmoke she was used to smelling. "They're too pompous."

Rune smirked. "You'd be surprised. There are rebels in each quarter, you know."

"So you say," Cove said. Theo's hand tightened on her forearm in a silent warning she knew well, and she sighed, turning toward him. "What?" Surely, he didn't have a rebuke for her. She was right, after all. They'd kill Theo on the spot if they saw him, and especially if they noticed his blindness.

"I don't think anyone's worthy of following Iosua," he mumbled, staring ahead into nothing. "I think it's his goodness that makes us follow, not where we're from or what we deserve. That's what makes him different than Solmere's deities."

A retort was fresh on Cove's tongue when she felt the burning in her black stains, changed course, and buried it deep. Would she harbor and multiply her resentment for these people and put her own life at risk? Or would she show a little self control and make sure her death really counted for the people she loved? If Arne and Ingrid could point her to Iosua and the cure, she'd swallow her pride and accept help. Maybe.

"Fine," she huffed. "I suppose you're right."

"I know I am," he said, but his tone wasn't angry. It was gentle. Confident. She'd never seen him so sure. And perhaps that was what struck her breastbone so deeply. She patted Theo's hand with her free one.

Maybe he saw things more clearly than she did sometimes. Maybe he could see into a realm hidden from the rest, and that's why Solmere hated him—and people like him—so deeply. A selfless man with keen discernment would be the king's worst nightmare, after all.

"If you're done railing against the known world according to you, Cove, pull up your hoods," Rune instructed, droll. Her gaze snapped toward him, realizing he'd pulled his own to shield his profile, dipping down to shade his eyes. Theo fumbled for his, and Cove tugged hers up after she helped Theo with his.

"Now what?" She almost tacked on a 'since you know everything' retort, but withheld. Something about what Theo had said made her not want to explain any ill remarks to Iosua if Rune told him about her conduct.

Rune crossed his arms. "We walk with purpose but silence. Theo, you can't show that you're blind. They'll see you as a dead giveaway for a Black Quarter trespass. That means no following behind Cove or holding onto her like you do. The Gray Quarter is much stricter with their rules than what you're used to."

"But how else is he supposed to walk?" Cove shot back immediately.

"I don't know." Rune paused and a wicked smirk grew over his face. "Act like lovers. They wouldn't walk one behind another. They'd be side by side, engrossed in one another. So Cove, you play the part well, and whisper instructions to him while he's walking. Theo, you're going to have to play along like she speaks sweet nothings. Disgust will drive attention away from us all."

Cove glanced toward Theo and saw his ears, neck, and cheeks turn crimson. Was he ashamed? Embarrassed? Her face grew hot, too. But Theo nodded.

She sucked in a deep breath. "We can do that," she finally said, reaching to take Theo's arm and clinging to it like some of the desperate women she'd seen on roadways in the Red Quarter. She'd never seen her mother and father behave in such a way. But perhaps they'd been more reserved. Surely they'd once loved one another in such a way. Right? Or was love simply another myth, a fairytale to give hopeless children a light? She hadn't seen affection in Erik, not even as he'd attempted to charm her.

Was it the same way with Mother and Father? Had he bullishly forced his way into Mother's life? Or had they simply driven each other to hatred?

Rune rolled his eyes. "You'll have to play the part, Cove. You look *pathetic*."

"I am—I will," she corrected herself. It was just that she'd known Theo her whole life. The notion of this arrangement had never been entertained because children born with disabilities were not allowed by the king to seek marriage. So she had buried any feelings she may have had, and buried them deep. The royals intended to eradicate the Black Quarter someday through better breeding, Erik had explained to her at one point. And then she'd been promised to Erik, so she'd been preparing to seal this part of her life away. Knowing Theo was as natural as breathing to her. But now, she found it hard to draw in air.

Rune shook his head. "Follow me. Two paces off."

With that, they crept through the maze of tunnels and alleyways, wove around the back of a building, and slipped into another alleyway. The darkening sky overhead announced the sun's departure.

Cove tugged on Theo's arm, bringing his ear down toward her mouth. "There are two steps and more cobblestone," she whispered. He shuddered, but silently nodded.

"Are we heading for the pub?" he asked, dipping so close that his nose bumped her ear.

"I don't know. I only see the sides of buildings right now. They're tall. Stone."

He reached out a free hand and brushed it against the building. "People coming," he murmured. Cove looked around Rune. Sure enough, a group of rowdy men were raucously arguing some ahead of them. Theo cleared his throat. "Sorry."

"Sorry for what—?" Cove broke off short when Theo wrapped his left arm around her waist, placed a protective right hand at her right bicep, and tugged her to his side just as the men roughly approached, shoving into Rune.

They plowed past him and the trio's tight-knit group was broken up.

"Hey, back off!" Rune shouted a string of curses, and the men turned their backs toward Cove and Theo, walking backwards as they provoked a fight with Rune. Or at least, attempted to.

A man smelling strongly of spirits slammed into Theo's shoulder.

"Watch yourself," Theo spat.

"Or what?" the man asked, turning to Cove and Theo. Cove shuddered, thankful that the darkening alley would obscure the cloudiness in Theo's eyes.

"Or you'll find out who *I* work for," Rune responded lightly.

"This isn't between you and me," the man replied to Rune, "but the scrawny little man who thinks he's tall." Turning back to Theo, he drew out a small dagger from beneath his vest and played with it in the moonlight. Cove pulled herself to her full height, but had no opportunity to retaliate.

Rune cast a single glare toward Cove—as if she were responsible for Theo's actions!—and whistled, then pulled a dagger from his waist. That seemed to do the trick. Even in the dark, their faces blanched beneath black filth from whatever acrid odor took over the air. Theo kept Cove tight to his side until all was silent and Cove elbowed him hard.

"What happened to not drawing attention?" Cove snipped.

"Sorry!" Theo's tone suggested much otherwise. But still, she let him keep the arm around her shoulders. It was easier to lie that way. They followed Rune through a throng of sailors headed for port, a group of merchants herding goats home—meaning there had to be farmland somewhere in the dizzying maze—and another group of drunkards.

Rune halted abruptly, just in time for a side-entry door to slam open before him.

"Get out, you filthy Black Quarter!" a woman's voice shouted. "Before I get my husband!"

A boot sailed out the door, and Cove grabbed Theo's waist and pulled him backward two steps, lest he step ahead and catch a boot to the face. The other boot followed suit, and a burly man backpedaled through the doorway. Rune stuck a leg out and sent the man tripping and falling to his rear. The man never took his eyes off the scrawny woman in the doorway as he scrambled to his feet and ran.

Rune chuckled. "Good to see you, Ingrid—"

Her gaze landed on him harshly. "No time to talk. You have any weapons?"

"I—of course I do," Rune stammered.

"Then get in here." She glanced toward Cove, met her eyes. A chill rushed through Cove. This woman had just been speaking ill of a Black Quarter. What was she going to do with Theo? "You two as well. Be useful." She disappeared back inside.

"What's happening?" Theo asked.

Glass shattered, insults barked from within. Rune stepped around the discarded boots and waded inside.

Cove faltered. "Well...I think we're about to meet Arne and Ingrid."

SEVENTEEN

Theo

"Stay behind the bar," Cove whispered in Theo's ear. Her breath tickled the side of his face as he nodded. "Stay there. I'll come get you."

"Be careful," he said, though her absence was already marked by a chill in the air where she'd once stood. He sat down, pulling his knees to his chest. Frustration boiled deep down. He could fight. He'd fended for himself on the streets for years. But Cove and Rune didn't see that. They only saw a liability, someone to take care of. He was stupid to think otherwise. Why had Cove brought him along at all, if he were simply a toy to be discarded when the real battle began? Footsteps rattled the floor near him, jolting him in surprise. He was behind, presumably, the main drinking area. Was it friend or foe?

A thick hand wrapped around his arm, and the person dragged him to his feet. His head smacked off the bar in the meantime.

All right—foe.

"Cove's little plaything." Hot, rancid breath puffed against his face and he wrinkled his nose.

"And who are you?" he asked.

The man scoffed, and his identity clicked in Theo's mind. "A man who's about to leave without a trace. And you'll be mine to deal with, if I have anything to do with it."

Erik.

Theo's blood leached from his face; he felt it trail inward to his chest and pool. Even the life in his veins recoiled from this wretched man.

"I am not her plaything. And I am not *yours*, either. I will never be...and if I have my way, Cove won't be yours either."

Erik's grip tightened, and Theo tugged away from the man. Erik's focus—and most importantly, his weight—shifted to counter Theo's weak misdirect, and Theo brought his free fist around, smashing blindly and landing on the man's cheekbone. His fist popped, the man's face crunched. Stickiness dripped on his knuckles.

"You—" Erik roared incoherent curses. Theo wrapped his hand around the back of Erik's neck and brought the man down toward his knee, once quickly. It wasn't enough. Erik grabbed Theo by the waist and threw him. He clipped the bar with his shoulder, rolled, and hit the floor face-first.

"Theo!" Cove shrieked.

Shattered glass coated his landing spot. He scooped up a handful and found the base of a bottle still intact. As Erik's boots neared and his hand fisted around Theo's collar, Theo slashed with the harsh, sharp edges. Erik howled with pain at the same time as another man's scream cut off short. Theo stabbed blindly until Erik let go of his shirt and Theo managed to get his feet underneath him. He couldn't go into the fray lest he hurt someone like Cove or Rune. But no one else approached him.

And suddenly, it was eerily silent in the pub.

"Theo. It's me, drop the glass."

Cove.

He sucked in a sharp breath, letting the shard drop to the floor. Silence buzzed in his ears until her footsteps closed the distance, and then her hand was on his arm, bringing it down and pulling it toward her. He stumbled forward a step.

"Your hands..." she trailed off. "Ingrid, are there medical supplies?"

"You've a skirt, haven't you?" came the reply.

The rip of fabric filled the silence. "Cove, it was Erik." The only thing Theo could form in his mind: the men in control of Solmere knew exactly where they were at. Surely, that meant their journey was ill-fated. Unless they could find Iosua in a hurry. What if they knew about the Exiles, too? Would the rebels walk into a trap?

Cove's hands came back over his, wrapping fabric over them. The pressure stung, but he forced himself to stay still.

"I saw him leaving," Cove finally said, a tremor in her voice. "I wish he was dead."

"I—he said he would have you killed and—"

"I know." She paused. "Other hand, please." He raised it dumbly and she dabbed at it. Must not have sliced it open like the other one. He swallowed hard. Her gentleness in this moment was a shock against the harshness she faced the world with. "That's why I'm doing this, Theo. Either I die from the curse, and my life is meaningless, or I marry Erik and die, either from bitterness or from his own hand." Here, her voice broke and trembled.

"Did he hurt you?" Theo asked. She dropped his hand and he moved to close the gap. No more secrets. There was no silence as he waited Cove out, though. Rune joked with another man that Theo assumed was Arne. A woman's stride brushed by them, muttering about retrieving her boots so they could dispose of the bodies.

"Yes," Cove finally said quietly. "He always has...but especially recently."

After she'd helped him escape from prison. Of course. Theo wet his lips. "You can't go back, Cove."

"I know. Which is why I'm doing this. My life means something—will mean more when I'm dead. Whether in battle or as a sacrifice the cure may demand...but then you'll be free, Theo. I know it."

Her words punched him in the chest.

EIGHTEEN

Theo

SHE'D ONLY BEEN A tot when their mothers first brought them together to play in the grass—at least, as far as Theo could recall.

"Theo, it's Cove. Can you say Cove?" his mother had asked. Before she'd been bitter. Before it grew harder to conceal his blindness. Before his father grew sharp and impatient with the cloud that loomed over their family because of his curse.

Before then, he had known three things: gentleness, and his parents' love, and he had known Cove.

His mother had guided his chubby hands to touch the girl's face, and she'd cooed, reaching to grab at his clothes. She couldn't yet speak. But Theo could babble out. "Ob?"

"Cove," his mother gently corrected.

"Coeb!" He'd clapped, and the little girl had shrieked, giggling.

When Cove had grown old enough to walk, they'd paraded through the woods together, Cove showing him all there was to see, only through her descriptions. Now, he was certain that her words painted a world more brilliant than what could ever exist in Solmere, simply because it rolled from her tongue. But her own father had grown angrier. From the time she was very young, she'd spent more and more time with Theo, though his father grew angrier too.

And then he and Father had gone for the longest walk he'd ever been on.

"You'll stay here from now on." Father hadn't described anything, only tugged him along by the arm until Theo cried, sure his father would pull his arm from its socket. "You can't come home. They'll kill you. This is for your safety. And my family's safety. Maybe someone will take you in. Never know."

Hollowness had rung out in his voice.

Cove's father arrived some days later with food. He'd poured out apologies to Theo that he didn't properly understand; it wasn't Mr. Brandy's fault he'd been abandoned.

He was alone in the dark, without his Cove to shed light or even tell him where he was. People tripped over him, cursed and spit on him, told him to get out of the way. Nobody stopped to ask why he was alone. He was only six. Why hadn't anyone cared?

But one day, Mr. Brandy brought Cove. She'd wrapped her little-girl arms around Theo's neck and exclaimed how much she'd missed him. And then, nearly every day, Mr. Brandy brought Cove 'round to visit Theo, adding in the benefit of food and drink. Theo survived because of them alone.

But then the unthinkable happened. And even after her father's death, Cove still came. Every day. She spoke of Theo's family until she grew too proud to visit them; and at that, he missed hearing of them. His little sister he'd barely gotten to know before being abandoned. Perhaps they'd had more children to cover his absence. Another son to carry on the bloodline. One worthy to bear his family name.

Theo was tainted. Cursed by Solmere's deities because of some wrong he didn't even fully understand. But Cove never acted like it. She always said he was made of kinder stuff than anyone in the Red and Black Quarters combined, so perhaps the Black was better for it. But Theo knew better. Black was where you went to die. And it was because of Cove and Mr. Brandy that he hadn't. It was because of Cove that he didn't lose a sliver of goodness, and why he eventually began splitting Cove's rations with the needy little ones that were abandoned just like he had been.

He'd always known it: his world didn't exist without Cove in it. He'd always known he would never marry; his blindness would make certain of it. But in a better world where curses ceased existing at the hand of angry deities, and royalty didn't hand-pick marriages to purify their society...he would ask for her hand. Always. In any world, in every century, he would seek her out.

It was enough, he told himself, to simply meet with her on the daily. To visit. To exist with her. And earlier, pretending to be her lover, no matter how briefly...well, that was the easiest role he'd played in life. He just couldn't let it show lest he alienate her.

But now, an hour after leaving the pub with Arne and Ingrid in tow, he was still stumbling over the plot Cove had thrust beneath his nose.

She was willing to die. *Going* to die, whether by spite or sword or sacrifice. And she would do it for him and her family.

The only thing he had left to do was outsmart her. To speak with Rune and ensure that he would keep Cove safe so Theo could slip away and do what needed to be done himself. Somehow. Perhaps Arne or Ingrid could be convinced to follow his own plan. If it came down to it and he had to find his way, alone and in the dark...he would.

Nobody would miss his departure from this life. His family had been expecting it for his entire life. But he couldn't live in a world without Cove in it, and so he would not. He would conquer shadow and light and all that might try to take her from him, if only it meant keeping her alive.

He would give her the chance to see a better world. To prove to her what she'd always been to him: the one who painted darkness with beautiful color. He would prove that there was good, if she only sought it and laid down the bitterness that permeated the air in Solmere. If it was the last thing he did, he would be grateful to have meaning, finally, once and for all.

NINETEEN

Cove

Arne led them to a tall, skinny stone building and let them inside. Ingrid showed them up a spiraling stairway, so tight that Theo and Cove could not make it on a step together.

"Go ahead of me," she instructed. "I'll keep a hand on you and show you the way."

Theo nodded, head down. He hadn't spoken since the attack earlier. *Is he upset? Angry?* She pushed the concern out of her mind, focusing on his feet as they shuffled slowly up the ragged, uneven stairs. More than once, he tripped, and she grabbed his waist lest he fall on his injured hands. *Injured because of me,* she reminded herself. She should've done more to protect him.

Finally, they reached a small, upper room lit by a sconce flickering on the wall.

"Home, sweet home," Ingrid said with a flourish. "We have no food, I'm sorry. We also weren't expecting visitors. Save for one."

"One?" Rune asked. He took his boots off and chucked them by the stairs.

"Yes. Bo." Arne took a deep breath, shrugging off his worn coat. "He will arrive tonight unless he is captured."

"Who is he?" Cove asked. "And—well, who are you in this whole situation? Rune isn't exactly the keenest man for explanations."

"Apparently," Ingrid said, rolling her eyes with a smirk aimed at Rune, who immediately began arguing his case against Cove's own attitude. Ingrid focused on Cove. "Your dress is torn. Come, I have other skirts that might fit."

"No, I'm fine," Cove said. "My cloak—" She reached to tug it further over her shoulders and found one side loose. The heirloom brooch was smashed, with part of the intricate metalwork destroyed. She sucked in a sharp breath. "It's broken," she murmured, heart falling.

"What?" Theo asked.

"My father's heirloom." Her voice came out wispy. Pathetic. Her stomach churned and her throat threatened to seal off. *It's not the only thing I have left from him. I have his temper. His blood in my veins, his stains on my arms. Don't cry over such stupid things,* she chided herself, the voice in her head sounding for all the world like her own mother.

"But you came out with your life. I think that's a fair trade," Ingrid said. She came over and fiddled with the brooch a moment before her gaze flicked over Cove's skin, exposed by the loose cloak. "No fixing it, either. But there's no use crying over it. My, those are strong black stains on you, girl."

Cove bristled until Theo put a hand on her shoulder. "I'm sorry, Cove. But she's right. We got out alive. That's most important."

Cove bit off a retort. Of course that was most important. But without anything left of her father...

"I guess it won't matter, soon," she finally said on a huff. A pained grimace crossed Theo's face and she pressed her mouth shut. Why did it matter to him, anyway? She was doing this for him. If his curse was broken and he was made to see again, he wouldn't need her anymore anyway. He'd figure it out in time.

"How do you know Rune?" Cove finally asked Ingrid, whose gaze was bouncing between her and Theo with a sharp attentiveness. The woman gestured for them to sit on threadbare chairs while Arne and Rune took up watch out the small window overseeing the city.

"Rune and I met when a man named Iosua met us in the pub. This Iosua seemed like a man who would never set foot inside such a place. Too good to be there. And yet, he was seeking a young woman tormented by the darkness. He spoke of a cure for the curse the world is plunged into."

"Wait—the *world*?" Cove asked, brows furrowed in confusion. Erik said the deities of Solmere were responsible for curses. Nothing more, nothing less.

Ingrid nodded. "You don't think we're the only ones, do you?"

"N-no, but...our land is cursed by our kingdom's deities."

"All of the world is in darkness. The darkness is brought by the same powers, but we name them different things, I think. In our kingdom, they are Solmere's deities. In others, they're known by other names. Except, Iosua says, we won't be in their grasp for long. All it will take is one person to reverse this curse. He spoke of prophecy that many men have abandoned, which is why we haven't heard it yet. But Bo, he knows it. He's a priest with the Exiles. Which is why he's going to meet us tonight. A group of Exiles are going to meet Iosua in the Citadel. He says the time is approaching for the curse to be reversed."

Cove's brows furrowed. "He knows all this?" she asked.

Theo swallowed hard. "How does he know so much? He rescued me from prison. Somehow knew where I was. Showed Cove how to get to me. *What* is he?"

Ingrid's eyes sparkled. "He sees and knows more than man. He knows the appointed time is arriving. And when it happens, those black stains of yours won't matter anymore. That's what he told me."

"Ingrid is the tormented woman from the beginning of the story she told you earlier," Arne spoke up over his shoulder, a thick accent lacing through his speech.

Ingrid dipped her head for a moment, but nodded. "It is not who I am now."

"And Iosua...did what?" Cove asked, brows knit together in confusion.

"Healed me," she said simply.

Cove's mind spun. Healed her? Was Iosua a warlock? She'd heard of them, and knew the Gold Quarter employed some. Clearly, since they used sacrifices for longevity, they could do any number of wicked things without consequence. How would Iosua make a difference if he was more of the same? And if the cure was of Iosua's own design...her heart fell. Was it a lie, too?

Ingrid grabbed Cove's hand, as if reading her mind. "When you met him, did you feel different?"

"I wanted to crawl out of my own skin," Cove said.

"Really?" Theo piped up. "I felt...comforted."

Ingrid nodded, her gaze sliding toward Theo. "Black Quarter's got it, Cove. You felt uncomfortable because his presence calls out the darkness in you, makes it want to hide. He isn't a man borne of darkness. He isn't a man that bends to the demons of Solmere, but one who sends them back to their master, where they belong."

"Then what of him?" Cove demanded. "Who is his master?"

"To me, he is a savior. To Arne, he's a powerful man. To Rune, a change-maker. Bo will be able to tell you more about who his master is. What is he to you?" Instead of waiting for a reply, Ingrid patted Cove and Theo's knees, then rose and crossed to speak with Rune in hushed tones.

"What does she mean?" Cove asked Theo, scooting closer so she could speak quietly.

"I don't know for sure. But I can't deny what I felt when he touched me, Cove. I think he's one who can..." He trailed off, then threw his hands up in frustration. "I don't know. Make a difference. If there are uprisings, if there are men willing to stand for what Iosua stands for, if there are men willing to die for his message, doesn't that mean he's something different?"

“Or it means that people are desperate for change and will do anything to escape,” Cove said.

“You believed him,” Theo pointed out.

“I do still...I guess.” Guilt washed over her. “I’ve just let life jade me. I expect something will happen to strip this hope away too.”

“What if he knows a way to cure the curse without you...” He trailed off. “Cove, he might help you instead of you being a sacrifice.”

Cove shook her head. “Theo, no one has helped me in life. Never. Nor believed in me. If we see Iosua, don’t tell him my plan. Please.”

“If it means keeping you safe, I will. I cannot promise what you want me to.”

“What—” Cove’s heart stammered, a mix of betrayal and hurt rushing through her. But before she could puzzle out what he meant, Rune clapped his hands together.

“Arne and Ingrid, tell them how you’ve experienced the curse yourself.”

TWENTY

Cove

Ingrid poured water from a pitcher as Arne sat, Rune still standing watch at the window. "If Bo isn't here by the time the moon reaches the northeast, we're to go ahead without him and presume him captured and dead," Rune said.

"Wonderful," Cove muttered.

"So let's get on with it," Arne said. "Before we have to get moving." He glanced meaningfully at Ingrid, and she took a moment to sit, smoothing her skirts thoughtfully. Her blonde hair dipped to shield her face, and Arne laid a rough, thick paw over her smaller hand, staying her fidgeting.

"Arne and I are not married as per the king's approval, but under the Exile priests. My family chose a violent man for me, and I was wed at fifteen," she finally said, glancing up and meeting Cove's gaze.

"Early," Cove murmured. Theo nodded in agreement. A shudder ran through her as she remembered Erik's hands on her throat. They would've been wed for two years already, if she'd been in the same situation as Ingrid. She pushed the thought away.

"Yes. Early." Ingrid took a deep, steadying breath. "I killed him to escape."

"She did not kill him. She simply allowed it to happen," Arne disagreed. "He came after her. She ran into the pub to beg for help. He followed and tripped over the threshold. Drunk. He smashed his head into the stone corner of the building and was killed instantly. I was there to witness it."

Ingrid's face paled and she went to a different place. Cove could tell from the vacant expression that shrouded her from view. Arne swallowed hard, continued. "I was wed at nineteen, but my wife succumbed to the curse three years later, after giving me two children. Her heart was never in the marriage, and it embittered her. Ingrid and I, we had grown up in the village together and had always cared for one another. So when our marriages were both dissolved...well, we sought out a priest from the Exiles and asked for the blessing over our union instead of the king's fancy."

"Wait. You married without consent by the king?" Theo blurted.

Cove cast a quick glance toward him. She'd never known he was interested...in someone. As a Black Quarter man, he would have been excluded from marriage by law, though he was far superior to all the men in Solmere combined, even given his blindness. His inquiry stung. *Would someone else be his eyes?* Cove shook herself. *What's it matter to you, anyway? You'll be dead before you see it happen anyway.* She nearly rose to join

Rune, but something kept her there; namely, curiosity over the priests.

"Yes. They speak from the prophecies of old, the ones Bo is rehearsed in," Arne said. "They abide by the rules laid out in the prophecies, not by the king's law. They are to keep their whereabouts secret, though, because the king and the Gold Quarter would have them executed otherwise. It is an underground business for your protection and theirs. They have been underground for hundreds of years, since the last prophet was executed. It was not yet time for the Exiles to uprise, though there will come a day soon when the Citadel falls to us. And one by one, the kings across the world will bow to the one who conquers the curse."

Cove's brows furrowed. "I never knew...so much about the world. We aren't taught so much in the Red. Nobody expects us to make it long."

"There are Order of the Red Exiles," Arne said. "Near the eastern edge."

"I live near the west. Or...I used to." Cove picked at a thread on her skirt. She would never return, no matter how much she wanted *home*. "But none of that matters anymore."

"Nor will it matter once you meet Iosua again," Ingrid said, drawing herself out of the reverie she'd wallowed in.

Cove's head swam. Bo, an Exile priest, coming to help them. A woman tormented and healed. Could Iosua heal her? Or was she simply too...bad? What about Theo? Surely he was deserving. Arne and Ingrid had disobeyed the order of the king, kind of. Could she extricate herself from the pledge she'd been bound to Erik? If she survived...was there hope?

Theo had dipped into silence, too. But as she pondered these things, he nudged her. "If they escaped the will of the king...don't you think we—"

At the window, Rune straightened and shushed Theo.

TWENTY ONE

Cove

"There he is," Rune said, visibly relaxing. "Just Bo."

"I'll grab the door," Arne called. "Ingrid, pack our bag."

Ingrid leapt to her feet and scurried about the one-room house, doing just that. By the time Arne and Bo reached the top of the stairs together, she'd cleaned up half the kitchen.

His pale blue eyes flickered to Cove, then Theo, then Rune. He lingered on Rune, then shrugged his shoulders. "Good to see you all. I see we have new visitors?"

"Followers of Iosua," Arne supplied.

"We intend to see the curse turned back on itself," Cove spoke up. Theo shifted next to her and rose to his feet, then held out a hand for her to do the same.

"It's good to make your acquaintance. I've been preparing most of my life for his prophecy to come to fulfillment," Bo said.

"Does anyone actually *know* what the prophecy is, let alone who it is about?" Cove blurted.

"Yes," Rune said, annoyed as if expecting her to already know that. "Bo, tell them. Otherwise, she won't shut up."

The blood ran from her face, leaving her cold, though she couldn't understand why. She'd heard so many strange things this evening—the past few days, honestly—that it shouldn't come as a surprise that this strange Iosua could have prophecies about him. What if there were prophecies about everyone in Solmere? The whole world? At this point, she wouldn't doubt it. It seemed, more and more, that nothing which was done was ever a surprise. How could it be, when there were strangers who knew your name and told you the kingdom's darkest secrets on a random weekday?

Bo shut his eyes and rehearsed it.

"The One who conquers the kingdom bears the crown of Life as conqueror of shadow and light. The One known as El Elyon will send a Conqueror not to disparage his world, but to restore it from a perverse generation and the many which will come after." His eyes snapped open and he focused keenly on Cove. "We need to leave quickly. There were men following me. I fear they'll find this place."

"They already found the pub. Yesterday, I had Ingrid take the children to her mother," Arne said. He moved to help Ingrid pack up.

"Do you mean to think you're not coming back?" Cove asked. She shot a glance toward Rune, who simply watched from across the room. Her skin crawled.

"We don't know. At best, we will have to lie low for some time. At worst, captured and killed." Arne paused, glancing at Ingrid. "At least her mother was willing to take the children for now...or as long as necessary."

"It was the first time she'd seen me since I married Arne," Ingrid said to Bo, but glanced back to Cove all the same. "She was shocked, but accepted caretaking for the children. For both of our young ones. Five total, from our prior marriages."

They lived with multiple children in this tiny tower? Cove marveled. And swallowed hard. These people had so much more to lose than she did. Shame welled up inside her. It was ridiculous to worry and fret so much about her own life when others stood to lose more. She'd always been destined for death. It shouldn't come as a surprise when it came to seek her.

Theo reached for her hand and she took it. "We aren't leaving yet," she told him. "They're still packing."

He shook his head. "No, I need to speak with you."

Her brows furrowed as she studied him. His face was drawn, tense. Worry lines etched themselves across his forehead. "What do you mean? We need to be ready to leave. Unless you're second-guessing this? I'm not. Or do you not trust Bo?"

"I know you aren't going to back down. But..." he cut off short.

Rune heaved a sigh aimed personally to them. "Keep the idle chatter for the escape, children; we *do* want to get caught."

Cove shot him a sharp glance. Neither were children, hardly in the sense of the word. She was opening her mouth to land a retort back to Rune when Theo squeezed her hand.

"This can't wait," Theo said. He turned to Bo. "Is Iosua the one who will conquer the shadow? Or is it someone else? How is the shadow conquered?"

Bo pressed his lips together. "I do not know that, young man. He speaks of one who will overcome it. He only told me that I would know more later, if I followed him to the Citadel. Three weeks ago, he met me in the Black Quarter and told me to strike out for the Citadel on this day and bring all those that would come seeking Him. He told me he had some tasks yet to complete, and a young woman to assist, plus something about a boy." He paused. "Iosua asked me to follow him once before, and I refused to. Thought my position as priest was infinitely more important. But then I realized that this priesthood was always meant to wait for what Iosua was ushering forth."

Cove's head pounded with Bo's confusing riddles and she glanced back to Theo. "What do you need to say?" she asked. "This man..."

Bo chuckled. "I don't make sense to you right now, my dear. But I know I make sense to your friend. I can see it in his face. You will come to understand soon enough. Once we're departed and in the thick of woods."

There were no woods for as far as Cove could see upon entering the Gray Quarter, and would not be until the Gold Quarter. Would there? She didn't speak out against Bo, though. He chuckled as if, again, sensing her thoughts. "I know a way through the Quarter into the Citadel, my dear. Just follow and trust us."

"Not exactly my forté," Cove muttered to Theo, but he still stood beside her, pale and urgent-faced.

"Cove..."

She sighed. "I know. But it can wait until we're on the road, yes?"

He took a deep, steadying breath and exhaled forcefully. "Yes."

Cove and Theo took up the rear of their little group as they wove through the town in disguise. In the darkness of night, there was no need to pretend as they had done before; the townspeople were in their beds, sleeping. As far as their group was concerned, there were no other people to see them except for the men Bo said were coming with orders for his arrest. He'd assured them that the men were perhaps a day or two behind him. Which meant they needed to put more distance between them. Cove barely wondered what such an old man could have done to capture the attention of the guards and mercenaries, when she decided it wasn't worth questioning. They'd arrested Theo, after all.

Speaking of...her stomach twisted as she thought about her friend walking just behind her. "What did you need to talk about?" Cove asked finally. Theo was as tightly-wound as a young colt in too much spring wind, and Cove sensed an explosion if she didn't give time to listen.

"What Arne and Ingrid spoke of. Their union without the king's approval," Theo blurted, voice low.

She blinked. Why was he so hung up on this? "Yes," Cove said slowly. "Are you upset with them? Do you think we shouldn't trust them? I think they were smart to evade the king's orders. I would want to explore that possibility if...things weren't what they were."

"It's not a possibility. It's real. And I need you to know that...I-I love you, Cove."

She wanted to freeze, but forced her feet onward with a nervous laugh. "What do you mean?"

They'd grown up together. Sure, she loved him as a human worthy of care. But any other feelings, she'd learned to tamp down. It was pointless to admit this right now. How could he be so certain? He couldn't even see her.

"I always have, Cove, and I don't want to lose you when you try to break the curse."

She shook her head and bit back a scoff. So it was all a ploy to keep her from seeking out the cure. That's all? "I'm doing this for you and my family," Cove said. "I have to. Why can't you accept that? Why aren't you thankful?"

"You're doing it to escape a life of rules that they've just proven are bendable. Breakable, even!" Theo exclaimed. Bo glanced over his shoulder at them.

"Shh!" Cove snapped. "Quiet, or all the king's men will descend upon us! Knowing our luck." It couldn't be true. Not of her. Theo knew how violent her father could be. He didn't deserve living with someone like her, should she grow so bitter in her own time. The warring emotion from earlier, the sting of thinking maybe he had someone else to love, and the pang of having to abandon Theo for Erik's self-interest, all balled up in a lump in her stomach. She wondered if she'd vomit. And most of all, she wanted him to stop talking.

"I'm sorry. But it's the truth. How could you assume I'm trying to derail you?" Theo shook his head. "You've never been able to see yourself the—well, the way I do. And no, I cannot see...but that does not mean I cannot hold affection for someone. I see by actions, in word, in deed...not purely the physical. Like your Erik."

My Erik? Cove opened her mouth in protest, then snapped it shut. "You know Erik wasn't my choice," she finally hissed. "And you'd do better without me! When the curse is gone, you'll be able to find someone you love and if the king falls, you can—"

"I already found her, Cove. It's always been you," he pleaded. "Listen for just a moment—"

"Please," Cove finally said, voice low. "Don't give me hope when I finally resolved to have none. Don't give me what I've searched for just as I give up the race. No one has ever loved me like that, and no one ever will. Don't give me false hope."

Theo's hand tightened on her arm. "Then let me show you before it's too late. Let me change your mind, let me prove myself and show that no matter what world we lived in, no matter who ruled over us, my choice would always be you!"

Cove shook her head. "Theo, stop."

He fell silent for such a long stretch, Cove was almost afraid he would. "Do you feel differently?" he asked, voice cracking.

"Theo, I've never even thought about it," she lied. "Even with Erik, it was forced on me. I never gave myself the freedom to wish! You know that!"

"I know that very well, and yet I have wished, too," Theo corrected her. "If you feel differently, just say so and I'll never speak of it again. But if you're simply looking for an exit, the one that hurts you and everyone around you..."

"I'm only fulfilling what my family has said about me from the start." *Let the blame fall on Mother, not me!* Panic welled within her. Of all people, Theo should understand!

"Then start listening to me and Iosua and the others that speak differently over you! Listen to the ones who speak life and hope and love!" Theo exclaimed. "You don't have to listen to them! Or Erik! Or any of the blasted kings of the world! Listen to me, Cove! You *choose* who poisons you!"

She jolted with his words.

A *choice*.

She'd never had a choice before. Did she now? Or was it simply one last trick before her life plunged into death?

Bo cleared his throat. "I believe this discussion will be aided by what the prophecy has to say. If I may intrude."

Cove jumped. She'd nearly forgotten about their traveling companions in the heat of the argument.

Theo forced out a harsh breath. "Of course." To Cove, he turned and added, "But please, think about it. This discussion isn't over."

TWENTY TWO

Cove

As Bo led them out of the town, he told of the prophecy and cure.

"At the creation of the world, man was made by El Elyon. He desired to walk with and love his creation, but man soon fell away in his hardness of heart, following the Deceiver instead. The Deceiver creates the idols and gods our Gold Quarter follows. It is believed that these are malevolent spirits, demons sent to steal, kill, and destroy. But El Elyon promised man he would send his own child to redeem the fallen creation. This man would right wrongs, would conquer shadow and darkness, and would wield light wherever he goes. He would appear to us all a man, but would hold all the authority and power of El Elyon. Through the ages, El Elyon has reached out to man through prophets and leaders we once numbered among the Exiles, trying to right his people and bring them to repentance. But none have accepted them, and all the prophets have been slaughtered. Ruthlessly. The remaining leaders and priests, like myself, have fallen to living in underground tunnels with the hope of avoiding a similar fate and preparing to battle the darkness one day." Bo fell silent and, likewise, a hush fell over the group. Cove didn't even have it in her to suggest that a creator above could wipe out the wickedness in the land with the snap of his fingers. Right? Or was it already planned?

Theo was the first to speak. "Why would no one seek the prophets who spoke light into the darkness?"

Bo smiled over his shoulder, illuminated by torchlight. "You are wise beyond your years, boy. Our people reject the prophets because of the darkness in our own hearts. It runs through our veins. Our pride refuses to admit that we are in need of saving. Our pride refuses to admit that we need a savior, or to forgive the ones who abuse us."

"It's stupid to do that," Cove shot back, finding her voice once again.

"It's *holy* to," Bo corrected sharply, and she recoiled.

"Why?" Her cheeks flushed with anger. He had no idea how she—and others—had been afflicted.

"It is holy to forgive and to love others because it is how El Elyon views us. We are in fellowship with him, and with whom we were created to be, when we follow his lead. When we forsake the ways of this world. Do you think the world would be better if others forgave and were not bitter, child? Would you rather set yourself free from the prison they put you in or would you cling to those bars and call them your own?"

She shrank into her cloak, tugging it closely around her, fingering the broken brooch. Would her father still be alive if it weren't for bitterness? Would he have been so sharp-tongued and angry?

Would her mother be wrapped up in her own anger and hurt if he had lived?

Would her grandmother still cry every night?

Choices... What would Cove do if she could live a different life? If she'd never been expected to follow her bloodline?

Cove finally stammered, "My father—"

"You carry the mantle of your generation, yes. But that is the curse you bear, none other." Bo paused, and she met his gaze, brows arched. "By that I mean, you are not cursed in the sense of the Deceiver cursing you to death. You are not cursed by a witch nor a warlock nor demon; and none are so powerful as to withstand El Elyon's commands. But you are cursed by your own mind and expectations, by that which was thrust upon you. You believe the lies that others speak into you, and so you bring it to fruition because you refuse to reject it. El Elyon sees you as pure and whole, Cove. Not as an angry girl with black in her veins."

"How do you know that?" Cove snapped. Theo tightened his grip on her arm.

"Cove..."

She spun on Theo. "No, I need to know! Don't you? Wouldn't you?"

Bo chuckled and she nailed him with a glare. He only smiled in response. "I know because I have studied all there is to study about El Elyon, and it is why I follow Iosua. I believe he is sent to tell us more of the coming time of salvation. When the curse will be lifted, broken once and for all. When we will be allowed to come to El Elyon and seek forgiveness and be healed from the sins and the ways we have lived. The ways we've gone astray like little black sheep. The prophecies speak of one who will give their life to reverse the curse of the stonehearted generation. One who will be mocked, scorned, beaten, killed. One whose heart is so pure, it will be clear to us all that there is a way to live selflessly, a way to live righteously, a way to live without condemnation. A way to forgive. A way to cast off bitterness."

Cove swallowed. Hard.

The only man she knew to be so purehearted was gripping her arm, fumbling his way through the uneven cobblestones.

Her heart turned cold.

Was that why Iosua went out of his way to free Theo?

TWENTY THREE

Cove

Cove dwelled on Bo's words long after he fell silent, satisfied that the others were caught up with the prophecy and how it related to Iosua. It still confused her. How could a man come from the heavenly realms to rescue such a perverted generation? Why would he? Why would any deity want to associate with them at all? If it were up to her, as the creator of an entire universe...she would've turned her back on this whole mess of a world, and as it concerned her, it would've been abandoned from the start.

And yet, *she* was dying and El Elyon was not.

Here she was, and there was Iosua in all of his goodness and all of the confusing ways he made her feel safe and feel like running all at the same time.

Was it the wickedness in her?

It would be easier to discern if she could find Iosua.

Theo cleared his throat. "What's on your mind, Cove?"

She jumped, startled. She'd nearly forgotten his presence—and yet, he was all too close. "I'm confused," she muttered after a few moments of stumbling over her words. It was all she could say.

"I am, too. But maybe we can talk it through and come to some semblance of understanding together. Rune and Ingrid have been, with Arne," Theo said, dropping his voice.

"How do you know that? I—your ears," Cove answered her own question with exasperation and he grinned.

Dawn started to crest before them, bouncing brilliant red and orange off the stone walls of the towering buildings, the maze they would tread until the Gold Quarter was within sight.

And then they would reach a spit of woods, or so Bo promised. She yearned to see it, even one last time. She sucked in a deep breath, wishing the air was tinged with pine and oak, not the sharp, tangy smoke coating the Gray Quarter.

"It makes no sense to me, why any deity would offer such a sacrifice to people who clearly don't wish to affiliate with him or do better."

"That's because we're most knowledgeable of the demons, not the angels," Theo said. "We're used to malevolence. Not goodness. Of course the realm of darkness would want us angry and dying. It makes sense. The stronger their kingdom, the more hopeless it is. See how hopeless we've been? Until we learned about Iosua, we thought our lots in life were to wait for death. And you..." He trailed off, but Cove nodded, setting a hand on his shoulder.

"I know. But it's got me scared. Someone full of goodness? That isn't me."

Theo's brows furrowed and he shook his head. "You heard what Bo said. You could be full of goodness if you followed Iosua and El Elyon. It could mean new life entirely. It could mean Rune wouldn't have to follow the life of a zealot. It could mean freedom for Arne and Ingrid. In the face of our kingdom, they are living illegally and could be stoned and murdered for it. For you, it could mean life, all because you rejected what others said about you."

"No...Arne and Ingrid would be imprisoned and taken for sacrifice. Same with you and me. So that tells me they're good and the Gold Quarter hates them for it, so as long as there's goodness to take...the Gold Quarter will continue thriving," Cove spat. "Which is why they need to be eliminated."

"I think El Elyon's son will claim his throne here on earth one day. Rune was telling me about it before," Theo said.

"Before?" Cove asked, brows furrowed. "When before? I've been with you the whole time."

"Not the whole time," Theo admitted, and his face turned such a shade that Cove recalled the only times she'd left him out of sight. Toileting breaks, which she'd pawned off on Rune, claiming it was unladylike to assist Theo with such matters.

Rune had borne the burden as well as Rune ever did...with much grumbling.

"So that's what Rune fights for?" Cove asked. "For an earthly throne for El Elyon?"

"Well, for the savior he sends. Yes. One day, it will happen. He said Bo told him, and he heard Iosua speak of it once. Just once."

Cove squeezed his shoulder again, her equivalent of a nod. "But I'm scared that the one who is whole enough, righteous enough, good enough...Theo, the only one I know, the only one here without black stains, is you."

He stopped, his face going blank. "Me?" he finally asked, voice small. "I don't know. I never knew..."

"Your fingers are black. That's it. You forgave your family, though I don't know how. You care, you're concerned about them. You never hold it against those who mistreat you. Theo, you're the most honorable person I know, which is why I always said your curse was ridiculous."

"I am cursed, though. My blindness means I'm not pure. Right?" Before she could answer, before she could ponder on the sudden relief that flooded her at his logic, he shook his head. "It doesn't matter. I'd do it in an instant, if it's me. But...just my fingers?"

"Yes." Cove reached for his hands as they walked, touching the line where the black ended and tan skin began. His face flooded red, and so did hers. "That's where, uh, it ends. The black." She shook off the sudden nearness. What he'd said to her earlier was getting to her head. That was all. She smirked instead, to create the moment irreverent. "So what do you think you ever did that was mildly wicked? What secrets do you keep, Theo Mikro?"

Theo choked so severely that Arne tossed a glance over his shoulder. "Is he well, Cove?"

She thumped his back between his shoulder blades. "Yes. I think he was just—I was teasing him," Cove explained as Theo caught his breath, wheezing.

Theo waved Arne off. "Thank you," he rasped. "I'm fine."

Arne chuckled, his barrel-belly jiggling. "I'd let off on 'im, lass." He winked and moved forward in the group.

Cove watched him leave, watched Rune's head on a swivel, watched Bo lead them fearlessly, his cane tapping out a pathway in the dawn. Soon, the alley would be flooded with people, unless this was a back pathway, a secret to most but the Exiles. Surely, Bo was leading them on the simpler, easier path. She didn't want to pretend being Theo's lover anymore.

Not when they teetered so close to the edge.

"Sorry," Cove finally mustered as she took Theo's arm and looped it back in hers. "Are you fine? I didn't mean to...to offend."

"No, that's not it." Theo fell silent then, and remained so until Rune announced that they needed a break.

Cove spoke to fill the silence, describing the towering walls surrounding them, the way the sun filtered through broken mortar and crumbling shambles where ancient structures once stood. Overhead, the blue, blue sky bespoke a beautiful day. How did the Gray Quarter survive like this? She couldn't stand it, not being able to see more than a few yards ahead of her. Neither could she stand Theo's sudden, stony silence.

What had she done?

TWENTY FOUR

THEO

BO LED THEM THROUGH the maze and out into a town square. Loud shouts, chatters, laughter, arguing—all a raucous mess that made Theo's head spin. Hooves clattered on the cobblestone, pulling a heavy load on wooden wheels that scraped by. The tang of smoke clung to everything. Theo could feel the sun on his skin and breathed a sigh of relief. Soon enough, they would be eating. Yes? That was his intent in bringing them out into the public eye?

He let his hand drift from Cove's shoulder. "I can keep up, I think," he murmured. He moved toward Arne's voice, believing them to be in the middle of the group. If he was in the middle, he couldn't get lost. He took careful, shuffling steps. Still, his skin burned in Cove's absence. He tugged his hood up over his head and down toward the bridge of his nose to hide his eyes.

"I know a pub off the path," Rune announced, and soon, Bo's clicking staff moved closer to Theo. He must have relegated the lead to Rune.

Time away from Cove meant a sickening sense of dread filled his stomach, along with resolve. If she only knew that he hid the secret of her father's death, if she knew that he was the reason she'd grown up fatherless, she would despise him. He knew how deeply her hatred ran, once it began. The well was deep and it could, quite possibly, drown her. She spoke as if her heart was near turned to stone, and she would know better than he.

It had been stupid to confess his affections toward her when he knew such an enormous secret about her family. He couldn't love her and keep that from her. Live a lie. But if he told her, it would be the last thing she'd hear from him, before she departed for the underworld spoken of by Bo. A world of fire and pain and anguish unimaginable. Hades.

He was a miserable dolt for having admitted his feelings for her. Of course she wouldn't accept him. And if she had, he would spend his life harboring that horrid secret, letting her live a lie. Truly, someone so despicable couldn't follow Iosua, could they? No one like Theo would be accepted by El Elyon. Not even Bo could tell him otherwise.

Salvation wasn't something he deserved.

He would die in darkness, in obscurity. And his secret would die with him.

Someone bumped into him from the right. Cove's arm snaked forward and she jostled into his side, stepping up next to him once again. She was protecting him. He couldn't bring himself to put an arm over her shoulder as before. It had been a secret joy before—some indulgence he'd never anticipated. But now it was a taunt.

Something to torment him.

How quickly hopes died.

"Just a mile's walk into the town," Rune announced.

"A mile?" Ingrid questioned. "We need to stay near the tunnels. The Exiles—"

"We will make our way back and save some time while we're at it," Rune said sharply. "Now hush. Don't speak of the Exiles in this place! You should know better, of all people."

Ingrid's light footsteps faltered, then scuffed. Arne spoke in low tones to her. Comforting.

They were so well-suited for one another.

How he'd wished to be an Arne to Cove.

Just earlier, Cove had told Theo he was the best man she knew to walk this earth. He scoffed at himself. He was the most honorable man Cove knew? If only she knew the truth.

It was his fault.

Suddenly, Cove's grip turned painful on his arm. "Rune," she hissed. "Rune! Ahead!"

Theo stumbled forward into someone. "Sorry," he mumbled.

"It is well," Bo reassured him. "What do you see?" he asked of Cove.

"One of Erik's men. I don't see..." she trailed off. A sharp intake of breath told him what he couldn't see: Erik was likely leading them once again.

Frustration boiled up in Theo. He hadn't injured the man badly, but if he had another chance...he would rather see Erik perish long before Cove. And if it meant protecting her, doing what he couldn't do for her father back when he was a child...he vowed then and there that he would.

He vowed to whoever kept and maintained vows. Himself? To El Elyon? He wasn't sure.

"Off to the left," Rune said, tone conversational, and the group slowly moved forward. "Cove, get to the middle of the group. I'll take Theo. We're heading into the woods quicker than I anticipated."

Suddenly, Cove's grip left his arm—shoved aside—and Rune's firm grip took his shoulder. Seized it tight. "They won't see her this way. Erik will be looking for her and I doubt he will forget your face," Rune explained.

Theo nodded. "Thank you." The tightness in his chest unfurled slightly. At least he could trust someone else to take watch over Cove.

"I know a way back to the tunnels from here," Arne announced quietly. "A better bet than trying to get to the woods, it's too far. Let's forgo a meal and keep moving."

Rune made a strangled noise of disagreement, but Bo stopped him short. "There will be opportunities in the night to seek food. We're nearing the business of an Exile, or we should be by nightfall," Bo reassured him.

"Couldn't have said that before?" Rune muttered, along with a string of other things under his breath.

Theo stiffened and he shushed Rune with an elbow to the ribs. "Do you want them to find us?"

Rune spluttered for a second, then relented. "You're right. Let's go."

They picked up the pace, until Theo was running to keep up with Rune, tripping over cracks and buckled-up cobblestone. The man didn't have the sense or care to explain what they were navigating, and Theo did his best to keep up and not be a burden. After a mile was well behind them, footsteps slowed. Heavy breathing. Sweat tainted the air. Bo, he assumed, wheezed softly.

And Rune's hand left Theo, instead pushing him forward. "Your girl's ahead."

"Rune," Cove scolded. She reached Theo in a moment, though he would've found her by the sound of her footsteps. He knew them well.

"Are you all right?"

"Yes, fine. You?" He'd twisted both ankles badly and smothered the urge to drop and probe them for any injuries. He would not slow down the group, nor would he worry Cove. He would *not* have her doctoring him.

"I'm fine." She sucked in a deep breath. "Just...I wish I could never see Erik and his men again."

"Me too," Theo said. "I'm sorry."

"Not your fault. It's all mine. My mess to clean up, and I'm just sorry you're all tangled up in it. I never should've made you come along."

TWENTY FIVE

Theo

The still silence of the tunnel system Arne and Bo led them to pressed into Theo's skull, somehow more discombobulating than the loudness of the Gray Quarter town somewhere above their heads. The air was damp, but somehow purer than aboveground. More musty, earthen decay than mercantile. The group huddled in still, stony silence as the guards, who had tailed them, neared and then disappeared. They'd evaded Erik's men once more. But how many chances did they have left, before their fortune ran dry and Erik's men caught up?

As Arne and Rune quietly planned their next move, Theo was left alone to be consumed with his thoughts. Cove's words surged into memory the promise Theo made to her father a decade ago—the promise Mr. Brandy never heard, as he bled out on the ground and was left, briefly, by the guards as they made preparations to dispose of the body. Theo had felt the man's blood pool against his shoes.

Just like now, he'd knelt on cobblestone. Theo had grappled for the dying man's hand, and clutched it tightly. So he wouldn't die alone. "I'll protect your girl, Mr. Brandy. Cove.

I'll keep her as safe as I can. Should I ever have the chance, I'll protect her."

With every breath in his body, he would keep that promise. It was a tall promise from a six-year-old, but he never forgot and he had always intended to keep it. That chance was now. If he was the sacrifice, though he was not convinced of it because he was no holy man, he would do it. Gladly. For her. And even if he was not the sacrifice, he would still do whatever it took to protect her.

She said it was all her fault? Little did she know.

She said he was in danger? That was a daily occurrence for him, and he would rather make do than have her disappear one day and never know what happened; never fulfill that promise to Mr. Brandy.

He owed it to Mr. Brandy. And more than anything, he owed it to Cove. Would the sacrifice only cover her, then? Or all mankind? He tucked the question away for Bo, even though he was sure Bo would point out that his blindness curse precluded Theo from being able to properly carry out the cure. *Granted, I've already been kidnapped to cure Erik's darkness,* Theo thought grimly. What if the sacrifice meant dying for Erik, too, if the man ever turned from his wicked ways?

What a confusing prophecy. What a righteous one. What a terrible punishment to take, dying for those who hated you. But what a holy gift, to die for the ones you loved—and those who loved you back.

Theo decided he didn't wish it on anyone but himself. Cove, certainly, least of all.

"Let's bed down for the night. We've been moving since before we picked you up, Arne," Rune finally said loudly enough for everyone to hear.

Exhaustion was dulling everyone. "I know another tunnel we can sleep in, connected to this one," Bo announced from somewhere in front of Theo. "You'll like it. It's deep underground and it's near to the Quarter border." Everyone hummed in agreement, and Cove tugged on Theo's arm, helping him to his feet and directing him to turn around and follow the footsteps.

"Steps," she quietly instructed, and Theo felt for the first drop. They were uneven, some edges sharper than others, and the steps were clearly hand-hewn and worn through time and use. After what felt like ages, they reached level ground. Dirt, from the sound of his footfalls.

"Stay here. I'll bring some food back from market," Rune said.

"I can go with you," Arne offered.

"No, you stay. Protect the others," Rune said. Theo hardly heard his light tread as he moved past, mostly just the breeze generated by his movement.

"I'm starving," Ingrid murmured. "How are you two?" She reached out and brushed something from Theo's shirt. A maternal move that choked his throat.

“I haven’t stopped to think about it,” Theo admitted after Cove murmured her answer.

“It’s a lot to keep up with, yes?” Ingrid asked. “The attacks, the prophecy, everything. Evading the prince, especially.”

Theo nodded his agreement, though his mind was far from the prophecy and Erik’s men and much more focused on how to best protect Cove while he still could. Whether he could at all. And how he could fit into this group instead of burdening it. He needed help to do it. Someone who would agree to help her once he was gone. Would Ingrid? Was it worth asking her for help, or would she scoff at him? He’d heard how she treated the Black Quarter man from the pub before. Was it an act, or her genuine attitude?

He couldn’t imagine her being so hateful. So maybe...she was worth talking to, after Cove fell asleep. Whenever that would be.

TWENTY SIX

Cove

Cove took off her cloak and spread it on the dirt floor. By her estimation, it had been a few hours since Rune left them, and he still hadn't come back with food. In addition to that concern, Theo had begun to sway unsteadily. She was impressed that he'd made it this far with only a few, brief rests; he'd normally spent his days sitting unless another Black Quarter helped him get to and from where he needed to. The only times he'd tried to navigate on his own, with arms outstretched, he'd been plowed over by a cart and then beaten by guards.

She'd found him the next day, bruised and battered. He'd talked her out of murder.

Now, she touched his elbow. "You can lie down on my cloak. It's not much, but..."

He shook his head. "I'm fine on the ground, Cove. I'm used to it."

She realized with a pang that *she* was the one unused to sleeping on the streets. Bo lived in the stony towers claimed by the Exiles, which were tumbledown by his descriptions. But they had to look unkempt, or the guards would be sent to investigate them.

Rune was a zealot who had no permanent home, like a nomad. Arne and Ingrid had their tiny living quarters, but she was nearly certain that if they had five children, those children would be bundled up in their single, small mattress.

Was she *privileged*, growing up in a house even if the house was full of strain and burden and angry yelling? Was she privileged to miss her bed and warm comforter, though it had holes and smelled of rodents? Her mother had envied the comforts Erik would be able to provide Cove, and Cove had intended to send goods and money to Mother and Grandmother. It was the only benefit she could glean from marrying such a man. And meanwhile, these people were living off of next-to-nothing and still had more cheer and kindness in them than Cove could ever imagine possible.

She sniffed, shaking the thoughts from her mind. "Well, I insist," she said to Theo. "Lay down and I'll wake you once Rune returns."

"Do you think he's run into trouble?" Theo asked, finally lowering himself down. She watched as he curled up into a small ball, his bony elbow pillowing his head. He looked so young in that moment. So much like that little kid her dad sought out and found one day after Mr. Mikro left with their son and came home empty-handed.

"I don't know," Cove said. "But he's a skilled soldier, I'm sure he'll get back to us unless he's killed." She sat, leaned back, and propped herself up against the stone wall.

"He will," Ingrid piped up. She moved over to sit beside Cove. She'd procured a small torch from the wall and propped it up near them. "There. So you can stay warm."

"Thank you," Cove said, surprised by Ingrid's care. She hadn't felt the comfort of fire for too long, and it nearly brought tears to her eyes. That was possibly the exhaustion, too.

As if reading her thoughts, Ingrid smiled and touched her arm, just briefly. "We all have to give up something to follow this prophecy to its end and reap its promises," Ingrid murmured. "But for now, rest your eyes while you can."

"What are you giving up?" Cove asked quietly. She watched Theo's chest rise and fall, though she knew better than to believe he was asleep.

Ingrid wiped her hands on her skirts, then smoothed them out, deep in thought. "I had to forgive the man who hurt me. I had to forgive myself for letting him die instead of helping him. Even though I despised him, it still broke something in me to see him that way. I was frozen, and when my mind caught up with what happened..." She paused, wetting her lips. "And now, I have to stay away from my children until it's safe to return to them."

"How could you forgive him? He was dead, it wouldn't hardly matter anyway," Cove whispered.

Cove watched Ingrid stare at the flame, her pale eyes distant, and was beginning to wonder if Ingrid had retreated into herself again when she finally spoke. "Because it frees me. From this." She touched Cove's arm, tracing a thick black stain that traveled up to curve around her elbow. "It freed me from the coldness, the anger, the bitterness that accompanies it. You know."

Cove nodded slowly. In the silence that followed, Ingrid added, "Arne gave up the privilege of being a soldier for the prison guard after he found out what the prisoners were being used for. You do know, yes?"

"Yes. Theo almost became a sacrifice."

Ingrid's face contorted. "I'm glad he is here still. He is a good man."

"He really is." Cove's stomach turned. "He doesn't realize it. His family despised him and abandoned him in the Black Quarter when he was a small boy." She didn't care if he could hear her. Suddenly, it became important for him to hear what she had to say of him. If either one were to perish...

Well, she would be comforted by knowledge that this had been spoken. The air had been strained and tense between them since his admission at Ingrid and Arne's tiny home, and she regretted the fact that her hesitation had created that wall. If they lived in a different world, a better one...would she still hesitate to marry him? It wasn't a matter of whether she loved him. She did, perhaps more than anyone else in this world. More than herself, certainly.

"It's criminal, what they do," Ingrid said suddenly, breaking into her thoughts. "The Gold Quarter. They don't have the right to kill and decide who is worthy of love and life."

"I know."

"How did you find Iosua?" Ingrid asked softly. She turned her attention back from the flame and searched Cove's face.

"Like you, I didn't find him. He found me trying to find Theo. I'd bumped into him once or twice before in town. But then he helped me rescue Theo and escape. He told me I would find him if I looked for him. And..." She spread her hands open and held them out, then dropped them to her lap. "Here I am, and where is he?"

"I suppose he is teaching and reaching someone else who needs it," Ingrid said, smiling softly as she leaned back. "If he told you that he would find you again, he will. Rest in that promise. When I get home, I want to tell my children all about him. I didn't before, but I should have. The prophecies, too. Do you believe them?"

Cove hesitated. Did she? "I wish to," she managed haltingly. It didn't feel like a sufficient response. "I just...wonder if it's too good to be true some days. Especially with as...dirty as I am." She'd never seen herself as dirty before Iosua. Pride told her everyone was just as wicked—even *more* wicked. But in seeing Iosua, and these others who followed him, she was coming to understand that same pride was her detriment. That same attitude cursed her, like Bo said. It was difficult, nearly impossible to unravel. And yet, she didn't despair in being dirty—she only wanted to know how to become clean.

Ingrid tipped her head, a smile curling her lips. "Perhaps you could speak with Bo if you're confused. If someone like me could be accepted and redeemed by this Iosua...surely El Elyon cares for you too."

"My family..." Cove trailed off. It was difficult. Would Ingrid understand her?

"Your family is not you," Ingrid said with a firmness that jolted Cove.

"She's right," Theo roused to say. "Thank you, Ingrid."

Ingrid reached over to ruffle his hair, like a mother, tender smile and all. The sweetness of it lodged an ache deep in Cove's chest. Theo had never experienced such gentleness. And yet, he was gentle. Soft. Loving.

His family buried him. And yet, he rose.

What was her excuse?

Ingrid smiled again, setting a hand on Cove's shoulder. "I'll let you think on that," she murmured, then rose and dusted off her skirts, retreating to where Arne and Bo spoke in quiet tones some yards off.

"You should, you know," Theo mumbled sleepily. He curled his hands close to his chest. "Talk to Bo, I mean."

"Maybe," Cove whispered. "Now, sleep." She rested a hand on his shoulder, as though he were a child who needed reassurance to drift into rest. He did, his face softening into peace as he slept.

Cove took a deep breath.

The prophecy took something from each one of them. But it also took the wickedness: Ingrid's sins, Rune's violence, Arne's sorrow and pain, she could imagine. And the prophecy cultivated it into something bigger. Something better. Something whole created out of the burdened and broken.

But Cove was a whole lot of broken and not much good. She wasn't even sure how she could live without the chip on her shoulder. Who would she be, if not for the living example of an angry daughter born to an angry man? Who was she, except the discarded girl who caused her mother to hold her breath through life, waiting to bury her own?

Theo began to mumble in his sleep again, and Cove prepared to set a hand on his shoulder, ready to wake him. But suddenly, his mumbling made sense.

"The guards...Mr. Brandy. They killed him, the food...pro mised..." His voice slurred with sleep.

"What?" Cove asked. She wanted to shake him, do something to quench the cold ice that shot through her veins.

The guards killed him for the food. The food? He'd been out to visit Theo...to take him food...Cove let her hand fall away from where it had poised above Theo's shoulder. He shifted, mumbled into his elbow, and fell back into deeper sleep.

She stared at him in silent horror. Did the murmuring make sense? Was it just a nightmare? Had it weighed on him so desperately that he dreamed of it too? Was it a lie created to cushion reality? She tossed her mind, wracked it to and fro, even though the memory was always in the forefront of her mind.

She'd clung to her mother's skirts as Mother opened the door. The loud thuds had shocked them from their noonday meal.

"Ma'am, your husband dropped dead in the corner near the intersect between the Red and Black Quarters. It appears he succumbed to the stone heart. We took the body to the undertaker. You will need to make arrangements to pick up the body after it's prepared."

He'd left early in the morning to run errands. After, he'd promised to take Cove to see Theo. She'd been expecting him home to do just that. After he got foodstuffs for their cabin. Grandmother wasn't living with them yet. Suddenly, it was just Cove and Mama. Her mother had dropped to the floor, sobbing. Cove had begged her to go see, that maybe he was only injured, not dead. But her mother's cutting words plunged deep into Cove's heart: "Hush up, child! He's dead, and it's his bitterness that ate him up!"

Soon, the accusations morphed. "If you don't obey me, you'll follow your father's footsteps!" In the Red Quarter, amongst the other children, she became known as the child whose father died so young from his stone heart. She would follow soon. They'd placed bets on when she would die, and she'd outlived each bet. Disappointed them all, she was sure. Some of the neighbors, including Theo's parents, even got in on the bets. It enraged her mother.

But how did Theo know anything about her father's death? She hadn't told him the details. She'd been too young to make sense of it herself. He would have been just a little older.

The intersect between Red and Black. The guards had found him there...near Theo. If they'd dragged Cove from that corner before...what if they'd killed him *right there?* They surely wouldn't have taken him as a sacrifice. But trespassing between Quarters was an offense worthy of death, according to the Gold Quarter. Had Theo witnessed it? Or had others simply told him? A sick combination?

It made sense. It made *sense!* An awful, gnawing amount of sense that felt like a death blow in Cove's chest.

"Why didn't you tell me before?" she asked aloud. But he had returned to slumber. She wanted to scream until he woke, shake the truth out of him. Fight with him. Something.

Anguish gripped her chest and she buried her face in her knees to smother the tears that crept forth. She hadn't cried in years. Hadn't allowed it. But that lonely, dark evening, she wept like an abandoned baby.

At some point, Ingrid and Arne approached and bracketed her, holding her. She didn't resist.

If her father had been killed...

If her mother's words were false...

Who was Cove, if *not* the spitting image of a rageful father?

TWENTY SEVEN

Cove

"Can you speak now?" Bo asked softly. The sobs had lessened, her ragged breaths lapsing into deep shudders. Ingrid had wiped the tears from her cheeks and fixed her hair, Arne shrugging off his coat and tossing it over her shoulders. But she wasn't cold on the outside. Just the inside, where no amount of comfort could reach. She fingered the oversized wool coat and sniffed, nodding dumbly at Bo. His eyes met hers gently, and he offered a hand. She took it, stepping carefully further away from Theo's sleeping form. Arne and Ingrid stayed close to Theo, giving Cove and Bo privacy. Cove almost wished Ingrid would stay near to *her*.

"What troubles you, sweetheart?" Bo asked. He searched her gaze. "You are perhaps the most troubled young woman I have met. And I've known Ingrid at her darkest."

"My—my father..." She trailed off. "He was a prideful, angry man. And we believe he died from the stone heart. But then Theo said something in his sleep—it makes me think that the guards killed him, it wasn't the stone heart." She poured out the details, every drop, to this strange man, collecting the pieces she knew and speculating on what she only sensed, deep down inside. "Am I insane?" she asked finally. "Is it...possible that he was murdered? Or is it some stupid dream?"

Bo nodded slowly. "I believe it's entirely possible. Do you trust Theo?"

Cove stared hard at Bo, confused. "Of course I trust him. But he was asleep—"

"Sometimes the truth haunts us in slumber. If it weighed on him, perhaps he began sleep talking."

Cove's eyes brimmed with tears. "I-If my father was killed...Bo, I don't know who I am. I became the girl everyone feared because I was stonehearted too. Father was no saint, but he...he wasn't *all* evil."

"Nor are you," Bo said patiently. "I believe you ought to trust Theo. Would you tell him if you knew his family was murdered?"

Cove opened her mouth to retort that she absolutely would, but..."I haven't checked on them in years. Theo asked me to keep updates on them for him. And I failed because I hated them so much."

"Your father's temper runs through you," Bo said slowly, measuring each word before they could pierce Cove's heart. "We can take after our parents. But it does not mean we cannot escape them. Turn bad habits into good. Or focus on their good traits and eradicate the bad, make sure we never hurt someone in the same ways they did. Theo has done exactly that, remaining softhearted despite their own prejudice against their son."

"But he's a better person than I am."

"Because you believed lies told to you by everyone you know. It's no fault of your own to believe people you should have been able to trust, but you are at the age where you can discern, rejecting evil and clinging to good. You are a prideful young woman, but you are also a broken one that can be healed. And El Elyon is the only one who can take brokenness and mold it into something new."

"When the curse is lifted," Cove cut in.

"No. Right now. In your heart, right this instant. As he did for Ingrid," Bo responded just as quickly.

Did she have black on her arms? Cove thought hard, but she'd only ever seen the woman with long sleeves.

"Pridefulness is a deep root to dig from your soul," Bo continued, resting a gnarled hand on her shoulder. "But it is quite possible. It is a lifelong process of laying yourself down and picking up the love and compassion of El Elyon. In his glory, you can lay down your pride in humility."

Cove's brows furrowed. "I don't understand." She wiped her nose with her hand and shrugged her shoulders in the coat. Maybe she was cold. And where was Rune? She'd rather think about something, *anything* else than tackle what Bo was saying.

"I will teach you, if you allow it. Or perhaps Iosua himself, once we catch up with him. But pride is an evil, sickly thing. It's like taking bitter poison and drinking it because you believe someone else is smaller than you. Or you believe someone deserves injury because they injured you. But drinking poison..."

"Ends in a stone heart and death." Cove bit her lip. "So pride hardens the heart. Not just the action, but the state of mind."

"Exactly. And humility softens it. That boy over there," Bo said, pointing over his shoulder, "is the most humble man you'll lay eyes on in this group. Learn from him. Allow him to lead you. Don't discount him."

"I never do," Cove said, bristling.

"Yes, you do. In turning away his suggestions, in rejecting his affections because you believe you are too far gone for him...that is pride, too, of a different sort. Still destructive."

Cove blinked, trying to keep up with Bo's words. "How? How do I...cleanse my bloodline?"

"Your father was likely a proud and angry man because he learned it from someone. It's a generational poison in your veins, to an extent. But it can be stopped when the person, the current generation, recognizes that it is no way to live. It can be broken by turning to El Elyon and repenting."

"If it's that simple, why do others continue to die to the stone heart?" Surely it was a trap. A fallacy the old man still had not noticed.

He smiled. "It's that simple in word, and that difficult in deed. Could you so immediately begin living a pious, humble life? Just because I told you to? Would you trust me immediately? Become a new woman instantly?"

She hung her head. Chuckled softly. "No."

"Then you have your answer." Bo reached and tipped up her chin, then settled both hands on her shoulders. "Dear one, you can be free to live." She sucked in a deep breath and he shook his head, silencing her. "I know your excuses. But do you see Arne and Ingrid? They live in rebellion every day. Holy rebellion. Following El Elyon instead of the one seated in the Citadel. I do, too. As does Rune. No one says you must marry Erik to live. No one says you will die because you cannot control your mind or your tempestuous tongue. Cove, you can be free. You can control your temper. And if your father did not die from the stone heart, that means you don't have to accept that as your fate either."

She swallowed hard. "There is a cost. Surely."

"Yes." Bo nodded. "It means following El Elyon. The cost is our own pride laid down. For some, that cost is too high. For others, they will lay down their pride *and* their life."

Cove dipped her head. The same tormented sensation she'd felt near Iosua washed over her. The desperation. The desire for help. The desire to scream out for someone to reach her. To *see* her. It welled up and her knees buckled. She knelt, Arne's coat puddling around her, and looked up to Bo.

"Can you teach me?" she rasped.

His pale eyes lit up, and he slowly knelt, leaning heavily on his staff. "This is how we pray, Cove. Repeat with me..."

TWENTY EIGHT

Theo

Rune arrived sometime late in the night, bearing some rolls and claiming he'd bartered services for them. Everyone had eaten their fill, and everyone remained subdued and quiet, though Theo hardly knew why. Rather than question it, Theo had dwelled on the fact that the rolls were the freshest bread he'd eaten since early childhood.

But the night slipped away and suddenly, Cove was shaking his shoulder as he struggled to wake. His legs ached to stretch out and he groaned. "So early?"

"It's nearly light out, and Arne says we can't risk being caught leaving the tunnel."

Good point. Around Theo, the others scuffed their shoes and rustled as they packed up. Cove set a hand on Theo's shoulder.

"Can we hang back a pace? I—we need to talk," she said.

Concern spiked in Theo's mind. "Of course." Was she upset with him? Or finally rejecting him? Was it about whatever happened in the tunnels while Theo slept? "I'm following your lead anyway."

Soon enough, the sunlight struck his face, warming him. It was something he relished after the cold, damp night. How it reminded him of the prison cell. How it reminded him of painful nights before he found his way around the Black Quarter. He'd tossed and turned most of the night, as much as he could recall, dreaming in turn about his parents' rejection of him, of Cove rejecting him, and the guards who killed her father—in his dreams, Mr. Brandy had died over and over again, and Theo begged and pleaded for help. For the truth to be known. Somehow, in his dreams, he could always see. But in the waking hours, he was reliant on Cove's directions, her eyes, her senses.

"You wanted to talk?" he asked, head tipped toward the presence on his shoulder.

"Last night, you were talking in your sleep."

"Oh? I was having night terrors," Theo admitted. "Sometimes I get them. I'm sorry."

"No, it's okay. Are they...do they happen because you experienced something?" she asked.

"Yes. Or sometimes, it's something that has not come to pass," he added. "Why?"

Silence wrapped around them for several beats. When Cove spoke, her words were slow and deliberate, tearing into Theo like the sharpest blade with every syllable. "In your sleep...you said my father was murdered by guards. Not the stone heart. You kept repeating it. And I-I didn't know if I should believe it or consider it a bad dream." Her voice cracked, and then the shuddery breath that came after cut into his own heart. He wondered if it was the wound that would finally end him.

The blood rushed out of his face and his limbs went cold. Should he lie? Tell her that it was just a bad dream? Could he live with the guilt? Or was this providential, that the truth leaked out just as he decided he couldn't face her? She deserved to know. Maybe it would help her see herself the same way Theo did.

She continued speaking in his silence. "I'm not angry. I just want to know what you know. Why you said that."

"I-I don't know why I said it, because I was sleeping," Theo faltered. When she said no more, he added, "But I do know it was true. It really happened."

Her breath caught. "Theo...you witnessed it?"

"It happened because he was bringing me soup. And the guards caught him and..." Cove's hand slipped from his shoulder and he reached for her, finding nothing. His heart clenched and broke. This was what he feared most, and perhaps he deserved it, but he could never tolerate the notion of losing her. "Please hear me out. I'm sorry, it's my fault and this stupid curse—"

"No." Cove sniffed hard. "No, that's not what I mean at all. I'm—all this time, we thought it was the stone heart. And it wasn't. I thought I did all my mourning already. But hearing it again..." She trailed off. "I'm sorry."

"No. I'm sorry. For keeping it from you." He reached in her direction, found her, and dabbed clumsily at her cheeks with his sleeve. "I'm especially sorry you found out the way you did. I should have told you. When you were—you were going down a path and getting so bitter over it, and I could have stopped it. Stopped *you*."

"No." Cove's voice was firm, though a tremor still existed. "Theo, I'm not blaming you. I just—I want answers. And if...if I get home again, I need to tell my mother. If she'll even believe me." She paused. "I'm...thankful, Theo. My mind is all muddled right now. I'm not sure I'll ever fully understand everything. But I'm thankful that he died doing something good. Honorable. He was a...difficult man to have as a father. But it means something that he cared for you. He showed me how to get to you. He was difficult, but he was still my father."

"I remember." Theo opened his mouth to continue, but she took his arm again with a sort of urgency, sniffing again.

"Please, no more. I need to focus on the task at hand. We *do* need to talk about this more thoroughly, but we need to catch up with the rest. They're not slowing down for us," she said with a small laugh. "Watch your step, there's a tree root."

"Thank you." Theo paused until he could hear the others around him. "I know you don't want to dwell here, but I wanted to say that I think I observed a side to your father that most did not, including you. For that, I'm sorry too."

"You have nothing to apologize for. It's who he was. A harsh, complex man. I suppose I take after him."

"Not only in the bad ways, though. And I wish you could see yourself that way."

"I'm…trying to," she said on a deep breath. "I spoke with Bo and Ingrid last night. About the prophecies, and how Ingrid was healed."

Theo's heart jolted. "Really?"

"Uh-huh. And it's…because of you," she admitted.

"No. It's something greater at work."

"Yes, but you played a part in it, I think," she said. "Really, Theo. Do you think you confess your darkest secrets every night on the regular?" she teased.

"Maybe if I had just been a braver man and told you, you wouldn't have found out that way."

"Well—"

"Shut up," Rune snapped. "I hear something."

TWENTY NINE

Cove

Cove pulled Theo along, aiming for a thicket of bushes. "Stay here," she whispered. "Keep your head low." She pulled her dagger from her waist and pressed it into his palms. "Only in case someone approaches you."

"You stay, too," Theo pleaded.

"No. I have to help. It's my fault these men are following us. And if I see Erik—" She cut off short. Would she be able to kill him? She thought so, but would it come at a price? Would she be forgiven, like Ingrid? Or was premeditation beyond the scope of El Elyon's mercy?

She shook herself and moved out of the woods just as Rune drew his sword. She'd figure it all out later.

"Here!" Ingrid shouted, and Cove barely missed the blade the other woman tossed her way.

Catching it gingerly, she moved in closer to the group, mostly to protect Bo. Her gaze skimmed the armor she could barely make out through the dense forest. *There.* She could see Erik's plumed helmet in the group of...at least fifteen men. Her heart quavered. Fifteen men? For just a few people?

He's scared of us, she realized.

Equal parts pride and terror flooded her veins and she gripped the blade tightly. The group broke into the same path that they were on, swords clinking at their sides.

"Halt, in the name of the king of Solmere. You're trespassing," a guard commanded.

"Yes. Near the Gold Quarter, I'd imagine," Bo mused. "A day's walk from the Citadel?"

Erik shoved forward through the group. "Who are you, old man, to speak to us?"

"Someone wiser," Bo said simply. He clutched his staff, but Cove had the distinct idea that it wasn't from fear or a lack of balance.

"Arrest them. But the girl is mine," Erik said.

His men moved forward, and Rune advanced likewise with his sword. "I told you you'd regret this."

Rune and one of the guards met swords with a bone-rattling crash. Arne and Ingrid bolted into the fray, followed by Bo. Cove watched as Erik slipped behind his men, his head whipping to and fro. His gaze landed on her, then skirted to the side. He was looking not for her, but for Theo. It boiled her blood. Good thing she knew how to affect him the same way.

"Be a man and come for me, Erik!" Cove shouted. She darted away from the crowd, the fighting, the swords and daggers. Someone screamed; not one of Cove's people. She snuck around a tree and met Erik coming around the other side. Cove's borrowed blade kissed his throat and he backed up a step, but chuckled hoarsely.

"Cove. Not dead yet?"

"You either." She pushed the blade forward, following him away from the tree. He put his hands up.

"You wouldn't kill an innocent. Not even you," he hissed. "A liar and a cheat."

"How did I cheat?" Cove asked.

His gaze flickered around the woods, still searching. "That cursed boy."

"Interesting that you consider him such a threat," Cove said between her teeth. "Suppose that says something about you. You *need* him, don't you? Admit it. You're nothing without the innocents you terrorize."

He bared his teeth and, quick as a snake, darted a hand out and grabbed her wrist, pinching a nerve. She dropped the dagger and bit off a scream of rage. If she screamed, Theo would come out. Instead, she swung widely with her free arm, aiming for his cheekbone. Once, twice. But it only stung her knuckles, and he didn't let go. Instead, he pulled her close to his chest and yanked her cloak back until the hem bit into her throat. She gagged and struggled against him.

"I want to see the life bleed from you," he murmured in her ear, and she cringed away. "You're worthless to me. To your kingdom. To your friends. What do you seek, anyway?"

"Something you...can never get," Cove rasped. She grappled for the fabric, but couldn't work a finger underneath it. He pressed harder. She kicked feebly for his shins, missing.

"Help," she croaked.

"If you beg, maybe I'll let your friend go," Erik hissed. "I see him just up ahead..."

No.

Erik tightened his grip on the fabric. Cove let herself go limp. He dropped her, foisting her body off to the side, and stepped over her. She laid prone, forcing herself to not breathe, until he was past her. Then she tore off the cloak. Her fingers reached for a downed branch. Grabbed it. Rose silently. As Erik moved toward Theo, she rushed forward and as he turned to see her, she swung. It connected with his shoulder, ineffective. But with the element of surprise on her side, she shoved him backward, kicking between his legs, and he finally dropped. Theo was on his feet in an instant.

"Run!" Cove screamed. "To your left!"

His feet shuffled in panic, but he collected himself and ran as she told him to. Toward the fray. It was a stupid idea, but hopefully one of the others would see and protect him. She hoped it was enough.

Before Erik could get up again, she grabbed the branch again and delivered another two blows to his temple. He went still. Before she could think about it, she dropped her branch, ripped his sword from his scabbard, and ran out of the thicket, driving the point toward another guard's shoulder. His breastplate deflected, and she slashed wildly, finally connecting with his fleshy arm. He dropped to the ground, howling. Just ahead, Arne was finishing off another soldier, but one man grabbed Ingrid from behind.

"Arne!" she cried, arms flailing. Cove was closer. She ran forward and slashed the man's legs. He shoved Ingrid away and spun toward Cove, and then Cove's face was splattered with hot, sticky red as Arne delivered his own blow, catching Ingrid in his free arm as he did.

"Let's run!" Rune shouted. Cove spun, searching for Theo, and found him still running—in Rune's direction. She raced to catch up with him, grabbing his shoulder.

"It's me, Theo!" she shouted. "It's me. We're leaving! Keep running!"

THIRTY

Cove

Erik's guardsmen left them flee to tend to their own, but Cove and the rest ran until Cove's chest burned and she coughed up blood. Only then did they slow down and take cover in a deep thicket.

Chest heaving, Rune explained the rest of their journey. "This is the last time we'll be in the woods. Once we step out, we'll be near the road to the Citadel. From there on, we must disguise ourselves. We must be careful. When we reach the edge of the woods, we will move in the darkness of night and hope to reach the Citadel's edge before dawn. From there..."

"We hope to find Iosua before then," Bo said. "He has answers. We need him for the rest of our journey, in all honesty."

"And if we don't find him?" Cove asked. This was truly the part of the whole plan that had fallen through so far: Iosua. Depending on him being there. Expecting him to meet them when it was most needed. But according to Cove, he was needed a few times over and still hadn't appeared.

The group fell silent, and Rune glanced around in a flash of annoyance. He shifted from foot to foot, and Cove practically read his mind—they needed to be moving. Now. But the others seemed to falter.

"We will wait for him. Here," Bo spoke, his eyes closed. "He will find us."

"He promised he would," Arne added.

Annoyance flashed across Rune's face, which Cove noted carefully. But he finally nodded. "Fine. For now...we rest. But only for the next three days. If Iosua doesn't show up by then, I'm going forward with the plan. With or without the rest of you." He cast a glance toward Cove as if expecting her to agree.

Something crawled under her skin, and she found herself shaking her head. A few days ago, even, she would have agreed with Rune wholeheartedly. But not now. They needed Iosua. *She* needed Iosua.

Why did Rune think otherwise?

THIRTY ONE

Cove

"May I walk with you for a moment?" Cove asked Bo later that afternoon as the group calmed down and rested. Theo had just leaned up against a tree, settled on the ground, arms crossed. He would be safe for now. Ingrid and Arne were speaking in quiet tones, and she supposed the woman was decompressing after the fright she'd taken earlier. Rune paced.

Bo's bushy brows raised at Cove. "Yes. Do you have questions?"

"I do."

"Private ones?" Bo asked.

"Y-yes," Cove said, wetting her lips. Not about her. But there was a gnawing feeling in her stomach that she couldn't ignore.

After they were several paces off, she turned to Bo. "Do you think Rune is a...betrayer?"

"Rune?" Bo asked. He shook his head, blinking hard. "I'm confused."

"Is he a traitor?" Cove repeated. "He was gone for so long while we waited in the tunnel. And how else are these men finding us? He said something to the guards when we were attacked..." But with Bo staring at her pensively, she couldn't recall what Rune had said exactly. And missing details wouldn't help her argument.

Finally, Bo chuckled rustily, patting Cove's shoulder. "Dear girl. I understand your concern, but he is steadfast both in his allegiance to the zealot order and to Iosua."

Cove bit her lip. "But it doesn't seem suspect to you?"

"Rune is always running to and from, orchestrating missions that he cannot speak of. If he seems troubled, it is because he has seen and executed missions that no human should ever do. It is not a mark against his person, but it cannot help but affect him. I believe that it what you're observing. He told us he had to complete a task in exchange for bread yesterday, remember? It could be that he was assigned missions to complete for the zealots that we cannot know of. Before we left, that is."

Cove nodded slowly, meeting Bo's eyes. He always saw so clearly. He'd seen straight through her, of course. So maybe it fell within reason that Bo wouldn't be fooled by Rune even if he was a traitor.

"But Erik's men..."

"Have been following you from the beginning, certainly. They are picking out-of-the-way areas to attack. They know the path we are on and they are using it to their advantage as they see fit. It's what his men do. It's what they have done for centuries, not only Erik."

Cove took a deep, shaky breath. "Is it me, then? *Because* of me?"

"Partly. They would still be after us, though, because of Theo. And you needn't worry. It's not your responsibility to stop them, nor your fault they are pursuing us. It is the fallen world we live in, the cruelty that these men operate under." Bo smiled and Cove wanted to believe him.

Perhaps she was too jaded.

Of course she was.

Shame flooded her at ever having doubted Rune. He was the one orchestrating this entire mission for her, after all. She vowed to put it out of her thought, and instead sought out Theo. They had some matters to discuss, too—her father.

THIRTY TWO

Cove

THEY WAITED FOR TWO days, and when Iosua had not shown up by the evening, Rune had announced he would leave with or without the group. One by one, they'd relented. And so they moved through the night.

"We're almost there," Rune finally spoke quietly in the early morning dawn. Cove's legs ached in protest, though they'd only been on the move for a couple of hours. They were arriving, just as Rune had predicted, near the end of the week. A day early, even, as far as she knew. Which meant they could get much-needed supplies from the merchants. At least through Rune, since he was a zealot and had connections. Or perhaps Bo? Were there any secret Exile farmers?

"Another half-day's walk to the Citadel, though," Bo clarified.

Beside her, Theo sighed heavily. "Will we cover it today?" he asked.

"As much as can be possible," Rune said.

"But a rest with my friends, in their upper room, would be sufficient," Bo said. "Weeks ago, they invited me when I said I might be visiting. We could move in the dark of night. It would be safer than anywhere else in the Gold Quarter, don't you think?"

Rune sucked in a deep breath, but Arne spoke up. "I think we ought to, and I believe resting before taking on the Citadel would be best."

"You're right." Rune relented. "Fine. We will dine with Bo's friend in the upper room, unless they plan to betray us into the hands of the guards."

"They wouldn't," Bo answered easily. "They are Exiles. Followers of El Elyon, and dare I say, devout followers of Iosua as well."

"Wonderful," Ingrid murmured. And so it was decided.

"I hope you will invite me in your plans," a voice like caramel, soft yet rich, announced from behind them.

Beside her, Theo beamed. "Iosua."

Cove spun on her heel and saw the man who had turned her entire life upside down.

His face was more gaunt than she'd recalled. His brown hair was longer and unkempt, and his shoulders, though not broad, looked strong but thin beneath the thin fabric covering them. A gentle smile still greeted her. She didn't shrink from him anymore. Her stains burned in his presence, but she ran to embrace him.

Chuckling raspily, he wrapped his arms around her and held on until she let go first.

"We looked for you. Theo and I," she explained. She would not accuse him, but it still struck her odd that he would tell her to seek him when he was about to disappear.

"Yes. I told you that you would find me. And you found the ones I hoped you would," he said, taking in the group at large before he turned back and smiled softly at Cove.

Rune nodded, loosening his grip on the sword at his side.

"I believe I am heading to the same location Bo spoke of. An Exile man named Marc will be hosting us—myself and my students—this evening, and I would like you to join us if at all possible."

Cove glanced toward Theo. His brows raised marginally as he turned in Iosua's general direction. *Students? Of what? Was he a teacher, like Bo? A priest?*

"Then we will follow you," Rune said, dipping his head in relegation.

Iosua clapped his hands together. "Wonderful. It has been too long since I've had a good meal. What about you?"

Murmurs of agreement came up around the group, and Ingrid moved to embrace Iosua as well as Arne. He set a hand on Bo's shoulder as he moved toward Rune.

"I know my friends are preparing a feast of sorts. It is the feast of the broken lamb, of course. The one the prophecies speak of," he added with a meaningful look toward Bo. Bo's eyes lit up and he nodded.

"Of course. I nearly forgot it was the time of the feast. I have traveled for weeks to get here. To catch up with these ones," he added. "We have added two followers to your numbers, by the way. Theo and Cove."

Cove glanced toward Theo, curious. Had he given his life in the same way Cove had? What was the feast of the broken lamb? Why did Iosua stare at Bo in such a way? Her heart quickened.

"Rune, you may continue to lead. I know you are a fearless warrior," Iosua said. To the others, he added with a smile, "In other words, Rune will go stark raving mad if I lead at my own pace."

Even this brought a chuckle from Rune, which Cove believed impossible.

"Very well," Rune said, reaching to clap Iosua on the back.

And the group was on the move once again, slipping through the woods toward the open expanse that led to the bordering Gold Quarter.

"It's getting real," Theo whispered, bumping her with his shoulder. "Isn't it?"

"It is," she agreed.

They were almost to the Citadel. They had survived this far. They'd evaded Erik and his men, perhaps delaying them for their injuries sustained prior. They'd found Iosua—or he'd found them.

Now, the cure.

Overthrowing the king.

And finding the conqueror of shadow and light.

THE CURE

THIRTY THREE

Theo

Dinner was served surrounded by some of Iosua's closest students and friends. They made a point to welcome the group, but Theo still stayed close to Cove. It would take one person to upend the whole evening, to turn them in and tear the dinner apart. The feast celebration itself told of something to be sacrificed. And he was a cursed man sitting next to a righteous one.

He still puzzled over being at Iosua's left hand, with Rune on the other side; if Iosua sought protection, he could not give it to him. Only Rune. At any rate, he took the food laid before him, quietly described by Cove as she settled a roll in one hand and his cup in the other. She kept near to his left side, so close he could hear her breaths over the general din of talking, singing hymns to El Elyon that Theo had never heard before. The music brought tears to his eyes, which he quickly swiped away. And the food was warm and fresh, something he hadn't experienced in years. He wished for the evening to never end. But as the meal indeed came to a close, Iosua finally spoke, and Theo could feel Cove lean forward to take in his every word.

"I know all of you, including my guests this evening, are wondering when the curse will be lifted. And namely, how."

Iosua paused and murmurs of agreement filtered around the room. Two brothers—as far as Theo could tell, having the same gravelly voices—bickered over something together.

"You must know the prophecy and what has come to pass. My friends have not heard the story in its totality. Have you?"

"No," Cove answered beside Theo. He reached blindly for her hand. He found it and she squeezed tightly.

"In the beginning was three: El Elyon, the Son, and the Spirit Above Creation. Through them, all was created. Without them, nothing was created," one of Iosua's students recited.

"Yes. And when The Deceiver corrupted creation, a promise was made, that the Son would cast out darkness one day, first for the people of Solmere and then for the whole world," another said.

"But the people were a stubborn, sick people, who installed their own religions and worshipped their own idols, sacrificed their children, and destroying the promises of El Elyon. Still, where the people were unfaithful, El Elyon remains faithful and just, and His promises will not be broken by the smallness of humanity." Iosua paused, and a hush fell over the dining area. "You may have heard the prophecy of the broken lamb, which we celebrate this eve. Every year, our Exile friends take an unblemished, perfect lamb and spill its blood, covering the doorposts of their homes with the product in atonement for the curse. Some of you have sought a cure from the curse for years. Some of you even believe and are willing to sacrifice yourselves for it now."

"I will die for you," a man with a raspy voice announced, and Theo flinched as a chair clattered to the floor.

"He just tipped it over jumping up," Cove whispered to him. She tucked a curl behind his ear and he shivered. Was she thinking of her promise? Was she planning how she would die? Promising herself she would be the conqueror? Or had she decided to stay?

"You will one day follow me," Iosua said, addressing his student who had knocked over the chair. "But you will also deny knowing me as your people have done for centuries. One even here will betray me."

The discussion rose to a fever din, and men argued amongst themselves.

"Should we run?" Theo asked in Cove's ear.

She gripped his hand again. "I don't think so. Arguing is nothing new, Theo. But if it becomes violent..." She trailed off, and he waited expectantly. "Ingrid and Arne are not making a move to leave. If they do, we will too."

"Very well," Theo said.

Above the din, Iosua's voice boomed, and Theo flinched in surprise. "Enough! Let us finish this meal together. All you need to know, I will tell you. I and the Father, El Elyon, are one. I am the Son, the one sent to vanquish the curse. I am the one sent to conquer shadow and light, and very soon, I will realize its completion. I will wear the crown called Life. I am your broken lamb, once and for all."

Cove dropped Theo's hand.

"No," she whispered.

"The one who betrays me into the Deceiver's hand, he must go now. Do as your master tells you," Iosua commanded. Bickering rose up again until Theo couldn't hear whose feet trod away. Chances were, it was one of his argumentative men.

But...Iosua was the sacrifice?

A pure man. A righteous man...

Grief welled up inside him. "He can't be the one," Theo said to himself. "Cove?" When nothing responded, he reached for her chair and found empty air.

"Cove!"

THIRTY FOUR

Cove

Cove bolted from the room, anger and confusion swirling around her. Down the stone stairs, out into the cold night air. She sucked in a sharp breath.

Confusion. Pain. Anger. Fear. Worry. Relief.

She was not the sacrifice. And from the sounds of it, if she sacrificed herself, it wouldn't be enough.

But if she wasn't to die...who was she? The fate of an early death had been pressed upon her from the time she was six, and she thought she'd finally found a way to make it matter. To be *important.*

And even worse, Iosua didn't deserve this.

Why would a loving El Elyon send his own beloved to be sacrificed? Wasn't it the same as the perverse sacrifices the Gold Quarter committed constantly?

But even better...it wasn't Theo, either.

And for that, she swayed and leaned up against the stone building in relief. She felt ready to vomit with the conflicting, swirling emotions polluting her stomach.

"Cove?" a quiet voice asked.

Ingrid. She reached for Ingrid's small, tense hands as she descended the last two stairs. "I'm sorry for causing concern, if I did," Cove said.

"Of course you did," Ingrid said. "Some of his men believe *you're* the Deceiver, even."

Cove scoffed. "If anything, I'd ask if Iosua is *my* deceiver. I was to be the sacrifice. Not him. I thought that's how it was going to be all along. It's all I could dream of doing with my life—to do something with meaning. And now that's been stripped away. And I don't know how to feel."

Ingrid chuckled softly, in a matronly way that made Cove's heart ache. How she yearned for simpler times when she had been loved. "I would imagine you might be relieved that you do not have to take on the sins of every person born," Ingrid said, leaning against the wall too. "Why would you want to die, anyway?"

"It's what has always been expected of me," Cove said softly. "And if I can't be who I am expected to be...what is the point?"

"Living is the point. Serving Him is the point. Loving others and showing his love to them is the point." Ingrid reached for Cove's shoulders. "Can I hug you?"

Cove shrugged her shoulders up to her ears and shivered with a sudden gust of cold wind. And only then did she realize she'd left behind her cloak, and her father's broken brooch, days ago in the attack. Her eyes welled with tears unbidden. She really had lost quite a lot. All of who she was. Her mother would be furious with her. Would perhaps turn her out of the house. And what if Erik caught up with them? What if...

She nodded, and Ingrid closed the distance, wrapping her up in her arms and pressing Cove's head down into her shoulder.

"Theo was scared for you," Ingrid murmured in her ear. "He's another reason to live. The boy is enamored with you. Say what you will about yourself, but he sees you the way you ought. Like a child of El Elyon. I will not lie and say that your path will be easy. Nor will it be simple. You will struggle, you will be angry, you will forgive, you will hurt and love and forgive again. But you must live to see it happen." Ingrid's arms tightened around Cove. "You must let go of what has been spoken over you. You must instead cling to what Iosua says of you."

"He doesn't know me—" *If he did, he would be disgusted.*

"I think he knows you, and all of us, far more than any of us know. Truly and sincerely, it is impossible to know what he does."

Cove shook her head. "I-I don't know what to do."

"In this next moment? Go back, brave the arguing of a dozen brave men with bullheaded attitudes, sit with Theo. Reassure him. In the next moment after that, soak in all that there is to know of Iosua. He says he is leaving soon. I do not know exactly what he means, nor where he is going. But a sacrifice...it means death, Cove. Know him for what short time you have. Do not squander it. You cannot change his mind. And in the moment after that, you will still have me, Theo, Arne, and everyone. I promise."

Cove hugged her back, then let go. "Thank you, Ingrid."

"Of course." She smiled sadly, tsking her tongue. "Now, let's go back in."

The women moved for the stairs, but were stopped by a shouted order.

"Halt! Cove, stop right there."

Her blood chilled her to the core and in that moment, she'd wished more than anything she had just stayed inside.

THIRTY FIVE

Cove

"Your time's up," Erik hissed. His right eye socket was bulging and purple. He was alive, but she'd done damage in the woods.

Why did she cringe? She should've been glad. Should've been impressed at her own strength.

"What are you going to do? Kill us? When you've planned to all along?" Cove asked, laughing even though her nerves clenched every muscle in her body. She took Ingrid's arm and pushed her toward the stairs with a single urgent glance.

Go get him, she mouthed to Ingrid.

But Erik saw. "Go get whom? Rune?" Erik asked. He turned to his left. "Rune, come here. Help these women."

Cove's fists clenched, expecting a fight. Expecting Rune to finish it. Expecting Erik's taunting words to finally come to an end.

But Rune stepped from the shadows with a curt expression. And held out his hand.

"Rune, I...what do you—" Cove stammered. Where was his sword? Where was the fight he'd put up just days before against Erik's men?

Erik produced a pouch from beneath his armor. Coins clinked, muffled from inside the bag, as it was transferred into Rune's hand.

Fury and sorrow blinded Cove. She screamed. "Traitor!"

Iosua.

The prophecy.

Rune belonged to the king's master, the Deceiver.

Ingrid reacted first, racing for the staircase. In that moment, two things happened: Rune jumped the handrail to the stairs and beat Ingrid to the top. As Cove opened her mouth to warn Ingrid, Erik grabbed her by the throat.

"You're coming with me. And I'm not taking no for an answer," he hissed.

She spat at him and he recoiled, shoving her to the ground and wiping his cheek. As she scrambled to gain her footing again, he strode forward and planted a foot into her gut. The next kick snapped her head back.

Cove's scream, somewhere in the distance, rattled every bone in Theo's body.

Traitor?

Theo bolted from his seat. In the time since Cove left, Iosua and his closest disciples had withdrawn to a garden, while the rest cleaned up and went their separate ways, citing unrest in the Citadel and warning the others. Arne, Bo, and Theo had discussed with one another about the risk the Exiles were under, and how it actually furthered their mission. Chaos lent a hand, sometimes, and they planned to use it to its fullest extent.

But then Rune had pushed through the door. "We need to go. Immediately. There's a—"

"Traitor," Theo murmured. His stomach dropped. *Rune?*

"Let her go. Now," Arne commanded.

Let *who* go? Theo strained to hear, but chairs scraped on the stone floor as they were knocked aside. He jumped up, too, and reached in the thin air for someone. Anyone. But he was left alone.

Arne. "You get Cove, I'll—"

A meaty thud.

"...Ingrid—and—"

"...Where's Theo?"

"Don't worry about it!"

"I'm here!" Theo tripped over a chair and went sprawling. "Wait for me!" he cried out, disentangling himself from the wood rungs.

Arne shouted, voice softened by distance. "It's a trick! Go back—"

Cold manacles slapped onto Theo's wrists.

"Stand up, Theo. I have the chair out of the way." Rune's authoritative voice commanded. Theo fought and lunged against him. When that didn't help, he began screaming Cove's name.

Her silence unnerved him. He kicked, bit, tried to headbutt Rune—until a well-placed blow struck him into darkness.

THIRTY SIX

Cove

Water gushed into her mouth, nose, eyes, ears. Cove spluttered, gasped, and choked. She flew upright, fighting against the grip against the back of her head, tangled up in her hair.

"Good. You're not dead. I want you to watch."

Erik.

Her veins ignited with fire. "I hate you!" she shrieked. "Where's Theo? Where's Iosua and Bo and—"

"We're here. Bo and I are here, Cove," Arne's voice called from some dark place. She fought against Erik's grasp to see, and he steered her face toward the dark corner where Bo and Arne sat, bleeding but alive. And chained.

"Calm down, Cove," Bo warned. "Remember whose you are."

Erik yanked Cove's chin, forcing her to face him instead. "Yes, remember, Cove. You're mine to do with as I please. You thought you could seek someone else, but it turns out I'm in control either way. And Iosua and his men just lost. Thanks to you. Thanks to Theo."

"No! Get his name out of your mouth, you coward!" Cove struggled against him and he let go abruptly. She slammed the stone floor on all fours. Her head pounded and she squeezed her eyes shut, gasping. Her heart was aflame with rage. Her stomach hurt. Her sides. Her head throbbed. Her stains—she gasped as a burning entered her collarbone. No. She'd come too far to commit herself to death in this way. She wouldn't die like a coward, bitter and hateful.

She would rather die like her father *truly had*. Protecting someone innocent.

A bleary thought entered her mind, swimming with lack of sleep, throbbing pain, and confusion brought on from Erik's earlier attack. *Maybe I am my father's daughter after all.* Maybe she wasn't nobody. Maybe it meant something more now, Father's death. He died protecting her whole world...she just hadn't known it until just now.

But what had the others done to protect Theo? Clearly nothing!

"Cove! Look at me," Bo commanded. His voice was so unusually authoritative that she looked up. "Look at me. Focus on me."

"No!" she cried. "What went wrong?" They should have been looking out for Theo. She'd expected them to all along, through this whole journey. She'd trusted Rune...Until she hadn't. And Bo had dismissed her. "This is your fault!"

"Cove," Arne's voice rang with a warning.

"No, it's *yours*, Cove," Erik said. He peeled a chipped fingernail back on his right index and flicked the sliver toward Cove. Trash.

Her chest heaved. Burned. She gasped as pain blossomed in her breastbone and drove her to her knees again.

"No, it isn't," Arne said levelly. "Cove...if Ingrid resisted, you can too. We'll escape and find Theo."

"Oh, they'll be long for the Black Quarter. Ingrid and Theo both," Erik taunted.

Cove watched Arne, waiting for the outburst. But Arne didn't look at him. He kept Cove's gaze firmly. So she kept his in return.

"Don't let him win," Arne murmured.

Deep breath. She forced herself to inhale as fully as she could bear.

She pushed away her mother's voice, saying she was her miserable father's useless, angry daughter. It meant more now. It would be an honor to die her father's death, with what she knew now.

Pushed away her village, who pushed her away first.

Pushed away Erik, who was now screaming in her ear. Or was he? It was only a quiet hum.

Pushed away Rune.

Put herself away.

Iosua. They had him. They had Theo. But if Iosua was taken...would he be killed before the prophecy was fulfilled?

Or was *this* it? Could El Elyon redeem this betrayal, or had the world just thrown away its one chance to be saved?

Her chest heaved, thirsty for fresh air, but the pain ebbed. She sucked in a slow, steadying breath. Erik scoffed, but she blocked his voice from her ears.

Arne nodded, and she finally saw the traces of panic, fear, pain written on his face. His wife was gone. His children, who knows where. Rune knew where they were, and that was worse than death itself. She was not the only one who had lost her world.

If Arne didn't buckle, she didn't have to bend or break.

"If you're ready, we'll get moving." Erik checked outside of what Cove assumed was a dungeon. A scream of pain met him, and he shut the door again. "Sounds like they're underway."

"Underway with what?" Cove asked.

"Iosua has been arrested for attempting to overthrow the Solmere throne and creating unrest," Erik said curtly. "He will be executed. He was tried overnight, and no word was spoken in his favor. He didn't even defend himself."

"He is meek and lowly, a man of sorrows," Bo whispered.

"So what? You want us to watch your sick tricks?" Cove asked, finally turning her attention fully toward Erik. "And then what?"

He chuckled. "Then, you're next. Rune will deal with the other two. I don't care about them. But I care very much about what happens to you. Come."

He unhooked Bo and Arne's shackles from a ring in the corner, and a long set of chains dragged behind each one, hooking one to another. Wrists and feet shackled. He clapped a set of manacles on Cove, too, behind Arne.

And then he took the lead, pulling Bo along by the beard. The gall; the sheer degradation. Cove's fingers curled into fists. Even though Bo hadn't listened to her...he didn't deserve this. He didn't deserve death for his mistakes, just like she didn't.

Arne glanced over his shoulder. "Control it, Cove. It's not worth succumbing to him," he whispered. "Trust me. Do you trust me?"

She wanted to bite out that she didn't want to. Somewhere along the lines, Theo had been abandoned. Had they run for her and left him, when she screamed? Or perhaps they had been split up terribly. Something had to have happened. Arne cared too much about everyone. He would never have left Ingrid intentionally.

The dawn was coming as they emerged onto crowded pathways. The screams had reduced to moans. And when Erik stopped them, Cove stood on tiptoe to glance around the crowd and she saw why.

Iosua was chained to a whipping post. A mockery of a crown, engraved with idols and the images of death and decay—similar to King Lycidas' own onyx crown—was pressed into his forehead, with sharp metal spikes that oozed blood. A torture device.

He made no move to protect himself. The crowd spat on him, kicked dust at his face, and placed bets on how many lashes he could take.

Why did no one do anything? Were the Exile numbers a joke? Just a rumor? Where were all the men that were going to take the castle? Did they care about Iosua, truly care? If they couldn't save one man...

Cove's knees buckled as the guard, in a garish executioner uniform, pulled back and lashed Iosua's bare back one last time. Flesh and blood trailed after the leather-and-metal strips. Her stomach heaved.

"That's enough!" a voice called, and hope sprang. Surely there was a mistake. They could help him, get him to a healer...something.

But the king himself stepped out onto a balcony above the crowd, smiling.

THIRTY SEVEN

Cove

"That's enough. We want him alive for the crucifixion," the king boomed.

Cove glanced up at the man, seeing the one who had been in control her whole life. He was an aging man, with gray hair and wrinkled skin. Black stains crawled up over his entire face, even soaking into the whites of his eyes. Terror flooded Cove's system. This was the man in control of Solmere. How many lives had paid for his life? How many children sacrificed, how many innocents' lifeblood had been poured out for such a broken, wicked man?

A shudder ran through her as the man's eyes swept the crowd. Another smile revealed teeth just as rotten and black as the rest of him.

"Get the others ready." With that, he turned and entered the castle once more. A moment later, an attendant arrived through the same door and moved toward Iosua. Cove watched, frozen, clenching her teeth at what must come next, but the man unfolded a purple robe and draped it over Iosua's broken, bleeding shoulders, then laughed.

"King of the Exiles, conqueror of shadow and light!" he jeered. The crowd raised the chant, and the guard unhooked Iosua from the whipping post.

Erik yanked on the chains abruptly, and Bo fell to his knees.

"Get up," he commanded.

Arne moved forward and pulled Bo up by the armpits. Cove followed close behind.

"What do we do?" she asked in Arne's ear.

He only shook his head. Of course, they couldn't speak now. But this was more than a covert attempt to silence her. He didn't know what to do next. And if Arne had no plans...

She swallowed her fear and kept moving. Shuffling, jostled by the crowd, head pounding and aching from the beating she'd taken. The sun rose and revealed three crosses on a hill. Behind them, an anguished cry.

"You! Pick up his cross," a guard ordered. A scuffle, and another man was dragged from the crowd.

Cove craned to see, sure it was Iosua's burden that could no longer be borne. A man grit his jaw and silently put his shoulder into the enormous beam, moving ahead as the guards jeered and spat on Iosua. He crawled on his knees until he fell again, and two guards grabbed him, pulled him upright, and pushed him forward as two other men walked ahead, bearing the weight of their own crosses.

Still, he made no move to defend himself.

Her heart broke with each step forward.

Where was the fight? Where were the Exile men? Were they, like Bo and Arne, silently moving through the crowd? Existing in the outskirts as they had for so long? Where were the men closest to Iosua, even? His students! Had they betrayed him, every last one? Cove found her cheeks burning with tears that wouldn't stop. Iosua dragged himself, inch by inch. And no one made move to help.

They reached the hill and Erik chained them to a hitching rail next to a guard's horse.

The other two men were already being nailed to crossmembers and hoisted in the air. The crunch of bones breaking, the agonized screams, chilled Cove to the core. She pressed close to Arne's back, trembling as she searched the crowd for help. For anyone. Anything. For hope.

The sun burst into clear view as Iosua was led over and pushed down onto the crossbeam. The nails were produced. The hammer swung. The screams wrought from him were mirrored by a woman with graying streaks in her hair. She clutched her abdomen, weeping in agony. She was held back by one of the men Iosua had dined with the night before.

His men were here. Why were they not fighting back? Had they no pride?

Or was this what must come to pass?

Cove's head snapped back to the men already suffering on their crosses as the guards heaved Iosua's cross erect next. A groan ripped from his chest. The woman wailed again. She and the man ran to the foot of his cross and knelt. No one moved to stop them.

"King of the Exiles, conqueror of shadow and light!" the crowds jeered as they moved past. Some spit even on Cove. "Follower of a rebel!"

She didn't correct them. None of them did.

Did time move? The sun did, slowly. Iosua spoke with the people at the foot of his cross. He spoke with the men suffering and dying next to him. The guards in the crowd fought and placed bets over the worthless articles of clothes other guards had crammed onto Iosua by force: the mockery crown, still crusted with his blood, and especially the king's own robe. It came to blows, but Cove hardly noticed them, even though Arne shifted to shield her when the roughhousing got to be too much.

To Cove, time stopped. All was lost, wasn't it? Without Iosua, there was no use in fighting against the men ruling Solmere. The wicked, wicked man that made her spirit revolt at the mere sight? He would win today, and all hope would be erased for the Exiles, for the zealots, the rebels...everyone. Erik would take her and kill her. He had already killed Theo, she imagined. Or Rune had. Ingrid and Arne would never come home to their children—if they weren't killed, too. Time stopped but the sun still grew hot.

Too hot. Sweat trickled down and mingled with tears that couldn't seem to stop rolling down Cove's face. Silently, she wept. For Theo and Ingrid. For her hopelessness. For the people huddled at the foot of Iosua's cross, watching someone dear to them be taken away. Someone innocent. Someone who never did anything but lift others up and teach them a better way; a better life. A righteous man.

She had never believed she would see one.

Iosua grew more restless, struggling to breathe. The end was drawing closer, she could tell. Not for the other men, but the whipping had taken a lot out of Iosua.

Was it a mercy?

He cried out and her heart ripped with it. The earth trembled at the sound.

THIRTY EIGHT

Cove

"It's real," she whispered. "All of it."

Arne didn't move next to her. He didn't speak. His gaze was latched on the man raised up before them. His ribcage struggled to drag in a breath. He was drowning on air. The man at the foot of the cross held the older woman at his side tightly. A few others crowded close.

"Surely this man was the son of the one they call El Elyon," murmured a guard beside them, set to post. Erik must have disappeared in the crowd at some point, Cove realized. She'd not even noted his departure. Perhaps the earthquake had startled him. Or he could not tolerate being in the presence of Iosua.

"He was," Cove answered the guard numbly.

Bo and Arne glanced behind themselves at Cove, and she shifted to stand closer to Arne. "Wasn't he? He is the Son the prophecy spoke of. This is his sacrifice. The one for all mankind, to right the wrongs we have done. To trample underfoot our Deceiver."

The guard next to them couldn't tear his gaze from the crucifixion. "Are you Exiles?" he asked.

"Yes." Bo's first words since the dungeons. "We are."

Cove waited for the guard to reach for his blade. To force them to their knees for execution.

He reached for his scabbard attached to a leather belt around his waist, and her heart skipped a beat, then sped up. But the man loosed his sword and it fell on the ground. "I have blood on my hands. I helped."

Cove shook her head. "We all did. We all did this. I think."

She craned her neck but could not see Bo's expression. Bo could ask the man to release them. To do something right. Maybe there was still time to save Iosua. Maybe it didn't have to be this way.

But Bo simply nodded. "We all did this. It is not your fault alone. You were obeying orders. But you may go and cease observing the rules of Solmere. You may join us."

The guard threw his helmet to the ground just as an ear-splitting cry broke loose.

"It is finished!"

Iosua's form went limp.

The sun disappeared, though there were no clouds.

An enormous crack echoed through the fields, and the crowds began to scream. They stampeded, tripping over one another in an attempt to get away. A puff of smoke and debris rose from the castle courtyard.

"The king's sacrifice temple," Arne breathed. "Bo?" His voice held a hushed reverence, but Bo did not respond. His head merely dipped toward his chest.

Chills coated Cove. And then a warmth spread through her. First in her heart, then spreading outward. It raced through her veins, then shot up her spine, and down to her very toes.

She faltered. "Bo...?" Now was the time to speak. She needed him, his reassurance.

"I feel it too," he finally whispered, then turned toward the guard. "Sir, you need to run. The other guards will be coming." The man, whose form Cove could barely make out in the darkness, turned on his heel and ran.

"Check him! Spear him, make sure he's really dead!" Erik's voice broke through the chaos, and Cove's heart fell.

So he hadn't gone far. And his footsteps were approaching. Cove shuddered as she sensed him coming close. Soon enough, his hands clamped down on Cove's shoulders, biting into her flesh.

"You're moving. Now. The castle was attacked." He paused. "This was all your fault," he added. He shoved Cove to the side and moved forward to unlock the chains from the hitching rail. No longer animals, so it seemed.

Instead of taking Bo's chains as he did last time, he grabbed Cove's wrists and dragged her, spitting vitriol with every step. "The curtain has fallen from the ancient temple of the Exiles. My father's sacrifice altar has crumbled to dust. The Exiles are doing something and I demand answers on who is responsible for this. I intend to get answers from you. You're lucky, else I would have had you three pinned to those crosses next!" he spat. "This is—"

"The work of a mighty creator above us," Bo spoke levelly. "It is the work of El Elyon. Nothing by human hands. You can hate and persecute and murder the Exiles, as you often do. But nothing you can do will ever stop El Elyon."

Erik gnashed his teeth and finally spat at Bo. "Don't you speak of him, old man! I know one of you knows what happened. It's what you intended from the start! Isn't it, Cove? Isn't it! That's why you tempted me in the square that day! You were always an Exile, you tempted me with your beauty and you knew I wouldn't be able to refuse...so you could get close to the castle and my plans against Lycidas. So that I would be destroyed! Without the altar, we cannot live for long. Without the altar, the king will fall in three days. Without the altar, so will I!" On and on he rambled senselessly, and Cove remained silent as he strode hastily. What use was it in rebuking him, correcting him? He was wrong, and he knew it too.

There was no use arguing with insanity, and Erik's rationale was dissolving. There was nothing to do except go to the prison.

And wait.

And pray to El Elyon that the others would escape safely.

This is where it ends, Cove decided to herself. But something like resolve covered her. She hadn't died in rage and bitterness. She hadn't died at the hands of Erik—yet, though she still might. Even so, something else awaited her. And perhaps she yearned for it. Would she see Iosua there now, in Life? If Theo fell into death, would she see him?

The dungeon came into sight, only by the lit sconces. "It's only noon and dark as midnight! That man was a powerful warlock," Erik muttered.

"The man was the Son of El—"

"Shut up!" Erik screamed. He yanked the chains and Cove stumbled, then fell before him. He landed a furious kick into her ribcage, still bruised and sore from his attack at their final supper with Iosua. She curled in on herself as pain exploded through her. "Get up, whore!"

She clenched her teeth so hard they creaked, then rose and staggered along so the others wouldn't be dragged down too.

Bo was released and dumped into the first cell. Arne, the second. Then Erik seized Cove by the elbow and yanked her, seething, for the third.

"I can't wait until I watch the blood drain from you," he hissed, spittle flying across her face.

She gave no response. For Erik, perhaps, that was even more offensive than her most ardent argument.

He snarled and threw her into the cell, and she hit the hard stone on her hands and knees once more. The door slammed behind her and locked. The best thing she'd heard all day.

It locked him out just as much as it locked her in.

Chest heaving, she moved toward the metal bars on the front of the cell and waited for the slamming door that meant Erik had left.

A commotion followed him; guards running away from the prison to help with whatever chaos was brewing in the streets. Finally, silence crept in and surrounded her.

"Are you all right, Bo?" she called weakly.

"Yes."

"Arne?"

His voice was shaking. "Yes. Cove?"

"I'm—"

"Check your arms, Cove. Right now."

"It's dark," she pointed out. Had Arne been injured? Knocked upside the head?

"The sconce, Cove! Now!" he barked.

She stretched her arms out through the cell bars, held her hands out toward the light, and saw the intricate, twisting pattern that she had known for her entire life. But it was no longer stained in black. In its place, a soft-glowing white emanated.

"He did it," she whispered.

THIRTY NINE

Cove

She sat, staring at her arms. Clean. Washed away. No more shadow of death. No more fear. No more curse. No more stone hearts—at least for those who believed in Iosua. Right?

It crashed over her in waves. Her guilt, her worry over Theo and Ingrid. Her desperation to see them safe. And the amazement that Iosua was the Savior, the cure, the prophecy all rolled up into one.

What she would have given to know him longer.

And Theo—were his eyes opened? Or was his blindness what she had always suspected, simply another symptom of the broken world they lived in?

"Are you all right, Cove?" Arne's voice came quietly. The guards still had not returned. Though whether it had been hours or minutes, Cove wasn't sure. There was no light and the sconce had snuffed itself out some time ago.

"Yes. You? Bo?" she asked.

"I'm well," they both overlapped.

Another prisoner took up chanting something that set Cove's teeth on edge.

"What is he doing?" she asked Arne.

"Praying to their idols," he said. "The Gold Quarter's, that is."

She drew back from the bars. "What should we do? Are we waiting for death?"

"Yes," barked the man who had been chanting. "Yes, for death, for the end of time, for the sacrifice..."

"The sacrifice has already arrived," Cove responded. He threw something—she heard the crash and shuddered—and resumed chanting.

"I want to get out. To seek out Ingrid and Theo," Bo said. "And I'm sure you both feel the same way."

"Yes. But how?" Arne asked. "Are they leaving us here to die? The guards haven't come back."

"They'll be guarding Iosua's tomb. Making sure the Exiles don't reanimate him or some sick perversion only the Gold Quarter would commit themselves," Bo said quietly. "Remember, Erik believed him to be a warlock? So that's where they are."

"And when do they stop guarding it?" Arne asked. "Tomorrow? Three days hence? Three centuries?"

"I don't know." Bo's voice sounded exhausted. Drained. Cove's heart ached.

"Surely, they'll come back. They wouldn't let us here to die, they would use us."

"Can they? Now?" Arne asked.

The realization dawned on Cove slowly. "Even though the curse has been reversed and their altar destroyed...they could rebuild it."

"Sick and twisted men are still allowed to roam the earth. Yes," Bo explained. "Would Iosua force you to follow him?"

"No."

"Then those who refuse to follow him will still exist."

Her heart fell. "I just want to get to Theo," she said quietly. "And my family has to know, too. They have to know everything, from my father's death to...well, everything."

"In time," Arne promised.

Silence coated the three of them for several long beats, and even the other prisoner fell into a hush. The darkness seemed to grow darker yet, and Cove decided it must have been nighttime. Which meant Theo had been missing for nearly an entire day. Was he dead already? What about Ingrid? She kept her fears to herself.

Scuffing broke the quiet, and Bo's voice came clearer than it had before. "We need to pray. Arne? Cove?"

"Still here," Arne said snarkily. "Prayer?"

"Yes. If Iosua was powerful enough to break the curse of death and stone hearts, isn't El Elyon powerful enough to reverse even this?"

Cove sucked in a breath. Was he? She discarded her doubt. Of course, he was. He was capable of everything. It was she who misunderstood.

Which made his sacrifice even more painful to think of. It wasn't by force that he had gone, but by choice. Choice and love.

Shadow and light.

Conquered.

For her.

And Theo. How she longed to tell him it was for him!

For all of them.

"You start," Arne said, relegating it to Bo.

Bo's voice came strong. "No. You start. I...I must repent." Bo paused, then began again in a softer tone. "Cove, I'm so sorry that I did not believe you when you mentioned Rune. If I had listened to you, or at least entertained you...we would at least be together. I suppose I owe an apology to you too, Arne. For Ingrid."

"You didn't know," Arne said, though his voice was tense. "Cove, what did you know?"

"I only had a hunch about Rune," she said.

After no response came, Cove was nearly ready to leave the bars to her cell door when he spoke up again. "Very well. Let us pray." He thanked El Elyon for provision, mercy, and glory. Thanking him for Iosua, his prophesied Son Above All. Imploring for the safety of Theo and Ingrid. And his children. Asking for miracles, for the spreading of Iosua's words across the world. Asking for deliverance. Asking for prison walls to crumble. Thanking him, again, for the veins that had turned white. For the second chance that had been dropped in their laps. Even when Cove didn't want it to.

The ground trembled. Or was Cove simply exhausted? She reached for her bars, but it ceased. Maybe it was her own exhausted and battered legs threatening to give way.

They prayed until a guard arrived with meager platters of bread and water that spilled as they threw the trays in. Cove lapped it up from the filthy floor with her tongue and settled against her corner closest to Arne's cell.

"It must be the next day," he murmured. "There's a sliver of light coming from the door."

"I think so, too," Cove agreed.

She fell into silence again, along with him and Bo. Two more men were dragged inside the prison, labeled Exiles. The day crawled onward, and Cove filled it with prayers as numerous as the breaths she took.

The dark crept in again, and the Exiles began to pray with them. The man praying to the idols was released. And so they began to pray louder and louder, until Cove's throat grew dry and cracked, and even then, she fell into whispers.

"You are above all, El Elyon. I know you will protect Theo and Ingrid and my family. I know you will. I know you will bring down the evil in Solmere..."

As dawn crept under the door once again, by Arne's estimation, the ground began to tremble once again, as it had done throughout the past three days. But this time, it began to shake. Then violently buck. She fell to the ground and covered her head as stones fell from the wall, dislodged from the mortar.

And suddenly, it was all still. Still, she trembled on the ground. When would the aftershocks begin? Would they be worse?

"Cove. Cove, the door. Get out. Come on!" Arne's voice, then Bo's, coaxed her.

She crawled to her hands and knees, trembling, and glanced up to see both men waiting. She blinked. Had she been hit on the head? They stood before her, and nothing stood between them. "Hurry!" Arne implored.

The other two Exiles were waiting, too. She pulled herself together, rose, and brushed off her torn and bloody skirt.

"What now?" she asked.

Openmouthed, Arne jerked a thumb toward the sunlight streaming through...the open door? Cove shook her head, ignoring the impossibility. Her prison door had swung open. Why *wouldn't* the door?

"There's an attack planned on the castle, and it may be underway," one man warned Bo. "Either join us or flee to the Black Quarter."

Cove glanced between them. Conquer the kingdom so no one would ever be hurt again, or go after Theo and Ingrid?

"Let's go," Arne said, pushing her between the shoulder blades. "For the castle. Let's finish this."

Bo's jaw set in resolve, too.

But at the top of the stairs was a set of locked metal bars much like the cell doors.

Arne rattled, slammed, and flung himself into it, but nothing budged it. Panting, he muttered under his breath. And then as he backpedaled for a running start, the gate swung open.

A man stood to the side flat against the wall, waving them through. "Hurry."

Cove ran out after Arne, nodding thanks to the man as she darted past.

"You are welcome, Cove."

She froze. That voice.

As the others pushed past her, Arne shouted for her to keep moving, but she was rooted to the spot.

"*Father*?" Her fingers trembled and terror seized her.

He stood there, just as she remembered him. Youthful face. A smile he reserved only for her, something that softened his usual stony exterior. Bright eyes.

"Papa!" she sobbed, reaching out for him.

But he shook his head, stepping back marginally. Her heart plummeted with confusion. "You need to go. And so do I. He sent me and a few others to help."

Who...? She glanced toward Arne, who slowed down and was waiting for her, but then it struck her. Iosua, in the heavenly realms. But if Father could come back...she shook her head. Why did he have to go away again?

"Cove," Arne called. She glanced back to Father, but found thin air.

Shaking her head, she dashed the tears from her eyes and pushed for Arne. Maybe she had imagined all of it. She forced her feet forward.

For the castle.

Ahead of them, fire burned.

The castle was already ablaze.

FORTY

THEO

TWO DAYS AGO

"Why did you do it, Rune?" Theo asked. Ingrid kept her arm looped tightly over his shoulders, and for that he was grateful. Rune had kept him cuffed, and chained Ingrid's feet together—likely to keep her from kicking; he could hear the chains rattle as they walked—but had unchained her arms so she could guide Theo. Theo was bound tight, and he had to wonder why Rune was so afraid of him escaping. Rune knew how impotent Theo was.

"I'm a guard for the Gold Quarter. And a zealot. The zealots grew tired waiting for Iosua to conquer the kingdom and Erik offered a reward for his capture *alive*, the same thing the zealots wanted. What else was I supposed to do?" Rune muttered.

Chains clanked. They walked along a cobblestone road. People jeered. Spittle hit Theo's cheek and dribbled down. He couldn't wipe it on his shoulder, not with Ingrid clutching him so tight. But he was glad he bore the brunt of the crowds' attacks, not her.

"We trusted you," Theo started again.

"That was your first mistake. Apparently, I'm a disappointment to everyone," Rune snapped.

"They're going to kill Iosua. I thought you followed him. Was that a lie?"

"I did!" Rune exclaimed. "I—at least, I wanted to."

"And you didn't see it through."

"You don't know what I'm doing. What I'm up against. I had to do it."

"No you didn't," Ingrid's voice came softly. Like a scolding mother's. "I trusted you. Arne, too. And our children...we trusted they would be safe. We trusted you with that information. Was that a mistake?" Her voice trembled at the mention of their children.

"Shut up, or you won't make it to the prison," Rune snarled, but Theo noted an instability in his tone. A waver.

"What, you'll kill us here instead of waiting until you have us there? What will you do with the other Exiles? You betrayed an entire community—"

"I said shut up!" Rune shouted. The town around them fell silent.

Theo wished someone would at least move, scuff their boot. Something. Suddenly, it was easier to breathe—which meant the crowd had dispersed away from them.

"I thought it was for the best. I thought I was bringing about the prophecy, the cure!" Rune exclaimed. His tone was tight, as if he was struggling to speak.

"What do you mean? By killing Iosua?"

Rune shoved Theo forward harshly, and Ingrid stumbled along with them. Moving so fast Theo struggled to keep up, he took them through a weaving maze until the bustle of the town grew faint. Then he shoved Theo into the wall.

"Rune!" Ingrid protested.

"I thought Iosua was here to overthrow the king of Solmere!" he hissed. "And when he didn't show up when I thought he was supposed to, I told everyone about it. When you all were in the tunnels. That is why I wanted to move forward into the Citadel without him. I thought by forcing his hand, we would be done with it sooner. I didn't expect them to kill him! What for, anyway?"

"For being a contradiction against the demons they sacrifice to!" Ingrid whispered sharply. "Of course they would, Rune! Stop lying!"

"I'm not lying!" he exclaimed. Desperation filled his voice. "Please! I didn't think they would kill him! Please stop!" Flesh slapped against flesh, but as Theo flinched, he realized it must have been injury Rune inflicted against himself. Ingrid didn't cry out.

"Then why are you imprisoning us?" Theo asked. "If you weren't on the side of the guards, why did you split us up?"

"I'm protecting you!"

"Why didn't you protect all of us, then?" Theo shouted. "Cove's out there with Erik and it's because you split us up!" Hurt and anger welled up inside him like he'd never felt before.

"Don't you get it, Rune? We trusted you to keep us safe! And here we are, still in chains, and you're holding the key!"

His voice echoed off the walls and an acrid odor stung his nose. Were they in the Gray Quarter again? Ingrid tightened her grip around Theo's shoulders—as did Rune.

"Don't hurt him," she said, voice low. "Don't you dare—"

"I'm letting him go. You, too." Rune's voice was detached. Defeated.

The click of a key. Theo's arms were freed. Rune sniffed loudly.

"You have to run. Back home. Run away from the Gold Quarter, you won't survive what's about to hit the Citadel if you go back."

"What are you going to do?" Ingrid asked.

"That's not up to you." Rune gave a humorless laugh. "You have made it abundantly clear that I have ruined much more than I ever could have imagined."

Theo swallowed hard. "Rune, if you made a mistake, you can—"

"I said that's not up to you!" Rune snapped. "Now go, before I change my mind!"

The clink of coins caught Theo's ear.

"Take this."

"No!" Ingrid protested. She argued with Rune for a moment or two before there was a soft thud, and then the clink of coins spilling out on stone.

"Just go." Rune ordered. "Now!"

Shing. Had Rune drawn his sword? Against Ingrid?

A darker thought crossed Theo's mind and his heart jumped into his throat.

Ingrid caught Theo's arm once more. "Come on. Quickly. Don't...don't slow down."

Her voice was rattled, and her hand shook. Theo obeyed without a word and they rushed through a cool, damp maze of stone until the sunlight hit his face again.

"Where are we going? We're far from—"

"We are returning to the Citadel," Ingrid said stiffly. "I have to look for Arne, and I'll look for Cove too. And Bo. If you'd rather stay back..."

"No. I'm coming with you."

She paused, and a grim satisfaction colored her next words. "I trusted you would."

FORTY ONE

Theo

The Citadel was in shambles, by Ingrid's description, by the time they arrived back the third day after Rune's betrayal.

They'd torn haphazardly through alleys and woods until reaching the border for the Gold Quarter, at which point Ingrid had stopped abruptly. She said nothing, having only stopped short, sucking in a sharp breath. Had they reinforced the border? Cut the Gold Quarter off from the rest of Solmere entirely? Theo wouldn't be surprised.

"How will we get past the—"

"There's *no* guard," she whispered. "Theo...there's no guard."

"No what?" Theo had asked.

"Come along." Her voice was urgent, and Theo followed without argument. "Are you good to fight?"

"Y-yes," he stammered. No, he really wasn't. If anything, this journey had taught him that he was more of an obstacle than anything else in true battle. But in a room full of enemies, he could at least assume whatever damage was being wrought on his enemy.

"I smell smoke," he said. He tripped over something and nearly pulled Ingrid down along with him. She grunted and yanked him upright. "What's going on?"

"The castle. It's on fire. The Exiles are..." She spoke in quick puffs as they ran. "Well, there's..."

She fell silent and stopped so suddenly Theo ran into her. She staggered forward as Theo regained his balance, muttering an apology.

"The castle's burning down and I think the guards have it on the inside, but our men, the Exiles, they're pouring into it. I-I don't know—" She shifted from one foot to the other, bumping Theo. "I don't know what to do. Theo?"

Theo paused, mulling over his response. Was he important enough to deserve the privilege of offering insight? What he spoke next would mark the fate of a mother, and that weight felt heavier than most things he'd ever carried. Without knowing about Arne's condition, Ingrid was all they had left. Assuming their children were even alive.

"If Cove is anywhere to be found alive...it's in there." Theo knew it in his bones. "And Arne, too. Ingrid, *I* have to try and find them. I don't expect you to go with me, because you need to get home to your children. You could go back like Rune told you."

"No. Theo, they'd be together. And I can't send you alone. You would die with no direction." She paused, and then a cool blade rested in Theo's palms. "Take this."

"Do you have another?"

"Take it." She refused to answer his question. "We're going right into the middle of it, Theo. We don't know how many Exiles are in amongst the enemy. Only attack if you're first attacked. You are more capable than you believe."

"Of course."

They began walking, and the chaos of the scene erupted in Theo's ears. Shouts, screams, the gurgling of dying men assaulted his senses. The sharp iron scent of blood. The vibrations of innumerable feet charging forward, slamming into their shoulders. The taste of smoke in the air, clogging his nose and throat. Then, the sudden heat of flame toasting his flesh. As they neared the inferno, Ingrid muttered under her breath. "This is ridiculous. This is crazy. This..."

"We have to try. Don't we?" Theo asked. "I'm sorry I'm in the way. But—"

"No! No, Theo, you're not in the way. That isn't what I mean. This is just...beyond my comprehension right now. I never thought I'd see the Citadel in such condition. I'll be all right. Are you ready?"

Theo was jostled to and fro in the crowd, but he nodded.

"Don't let go of me," Ingrid warned. "If you do, we'll be separated. Maybe forever."

"Of course." Theo locked his elbow in hers and they pressed onward together.

FORTY TWO

Cove

Cove choked on the smoke as she dashed through the castle. It was crammed with people, both Exiles and Gold Quarter sympathizers, so much that she could barely tell who was friend and who was foe. But then she came upon a young girl hunkered in a hallway, face covered with her stained linen apron. Screaming.

Cove faltered and Arne ran past, bearing his sword for the enemies before them. He would clear the way. She reached out and touched the girl's shoulder. "Are you okay?" she asked. A maid, likely for Lycidas. Who knew what she had seen, the poor girl. Cove guessed she was only seven or eight, by her stature and childlike face.

"No," she sobbed. "My mother, she—" The girl flailed her arms in the air and devolved into hysterics, shaking from head to toe.

"I'll get you out. I promise. Are you one of the Exiles?" she asked.

The girl shook her head, confused. "What's an Exile?"

Cove paused. *I can't risk telling her something she shouldn't know.* "I'll tell you later. I'll get you out safe. I promise. Do you trust me?"

She couldn't promise safety, though. But she couldn't let the child remain there. It's what Father would have done...wasn't it? She offered her hand to the girl and she slipped her trembling hand inside. "Hold on tight." If Theo was out of her grasp, she could still help someone else. It felt right and true to have someone to help.

She pulled the girl through the stone hallways, trying to find a safe place amid the shouts, the crash of sword against sword, fire, and blood-slicked floor. Where could they go that was safe in the entire Gold Quarter? She was more lost than the maid, certainly.

Screams above them. Screams below them. She rounded a corner and the smoke became blinding. "Cover your nose," Cove demanded. "I'm taking you out of the castle, all right? Somehow."

The girl nodded, tightening her grip on Cove as she clamped her free hand over her mouth and nose, and Cove picked up the pace. She darted through the chaotic mishmash of guard and commoner, sword and dagger. A thrown dagger sliced into her cheek and she bit back a gasp. Red trickled down her neck. The smoke lessened and she couldn't see her people anywhere. The thought struck her that she was going too far within the castle.

"The entrance is this way," the maid cried, pulling back.

"Thank you," Cove wheezed. She doubled back, pulling the girl along with her. Finally, the entrance.

And it was blocked by a dozen guards.

Her heart dropped.

"What do we do?" They were closing in, shields up and swords drawn, mowing the commoners down as if they were rogue strands of straw against violent winds. "Do we turn around?" Cove whispered, mostly to herself. Into the fire or into the swords?

The girl's panicked breathing worsened until her face turned purple. *Think, Cove!* She screamed at herself. To the girl, she commanded, "Calm down! Don't faint. We'll go through a window or-or something—"

"Cove!"

Her head snapped first to the left, then the right. *Ingrid?* She couldn't make anyone out in the mess of men and women and guards, a dizzying array of battle. The slick mess on the floor. Shing of metal on metal rang in her ears. Screams. Grunts. Dying moans.

Surely, she was hallucinating. The girl did not react.

Ingrid was with Theo. And Cove presumed them both dead. She shook her head to focus herself.

"There are windows that way." The girl pointed to the left.

"Then we'll go that way," Cove said. "I'll break one of them." She couldn't let her own hopes of Ingrid and Theo's safe return drown out reality. And right now, the only real thing she could be certain of was the innocent little girl clinging to her arm, who desperately needed rescue.

She shouldered her way through a crush of commoners who were retreating from the guards. Retreat shouldn't be an option. Would they give up the fight? After so much trouble?

"Wait! This leads into the altar room, and it fell down when they held the executions," the girl shouted. "Go this way!" Cove spun in a circle, confused, until she saw the hallway the girl was pointing toward. It led to shambles.

"Let's go. Fast!" Cove exclaimed. She broke into a run, and found more commoners pouring into the hallway. "When we get out, you run to the Gray Quarter, and you run fast. You know the path to Gray?" Cove asked.

"N-no!"

"It's south. The sun will be to your left as you travel in the morning."

The girl stammered out an agreement as they skidded into the shambled mess of the altar room. Cove's head ached as she entered the place, the hairs on the back of her neck rising. Her stomach knotted. Horrid things had happened here. Evil lived here. She stepped into the broken stone room and pushed through the commoners pouring through a gaping maw in the western wall.

"Make way! Make way! We have an innocent trying to escape!" Cove shouted, and men took up her cry. Soon enough, the movement ground to a halt and she helped the girl crawl through a hole up above her head, along with a wounded man who promised he would get the girl to the Gray Quarter.

"Run for the Gray Quarter!" Cove shouted after them. "Remember. Get as far away from here as you can!"

"I will!" the maid cried. And then she was gone.

Cove prayed for their safety, then spun back around.

Someone reached out and grabbed her.

She wrenched away with a shout, clumsily pulling the sword Arne had pilfered from a dead body and shoved at her as they entered the castle.

"Cove! Cove, it's me!"

Her heart leapt as she met cloudy gray eyes. She grabbed her whole heart into her arms and buried her face in his shoulder.

"I thought..."

"I thought you were dead!" Theo shouted.

"Me too!" She pulled away and he grabbed her face. His expression twisted as his fingers brushed the blood on her cheek.

"You're hurt?"

"I'm all right. Survivable. Where's Ingrid?"

"She went looking for you and Arne. We both did, and then we got separated. She told me not to get separated from her, but..."

"I thought I heard her!" Cove exclaimed. She sucked in a breath. The world was collapsing into chaos around them. The commoners outnumbered the guards now, surely. Even with the forces in the entryway. She pulled him into another embrace and kissed the side of his temple.

"You're all right," she said, mostly to herself. To him, she added, "Do you want to stay here? Or get in there and fight?"

"What's the end goal?" Theo asked. "What are they planning to do?"

"I don't rightly know. I know they want to expose the king. Erik is here somewhere. I-I...someone set fire to the castle. It's burning down."

Theo's face contorted, but then he nearly tripped as someone shoved past him.

"I'm going with you," he said.

"Very well." She tucked her arm through his elbow and he pulled her to his side, tight.

"Ingrid gave me a dagger," Theo added, pulling it from his belt.

"Keep hold of it," she said. "I'll tell you when we run into trouble."

He chuckled. "*When*, huh?"

"Yes. When."

Together, they pressed out of the broken altar room, through the hallway, and into the castle. Almost immediately, they came upon a group of soldiers pressing into the altar room. *Try and secure it,* Cove thought. *You never will.*

"Theo, the dagger. To your right," she explained. "Nothing but guards in the way. I have them on the left, too."

He nodded and pulled his own dagger, which seemed like an identical match to the one Ingrid had given Cove before. *Was she weaponless?* Cove wondered, panic spiking in her veins.

But to get to Ingrid, she had to focus on the peril before them. The guards drew their own swords, and Cove shouted, yanking Theo forward. He made the first cut with such efficiency that Cove startled. *Focus*, she told herself. *Cut. Slash. Do what it takes to get to Ingrid.* Some other Exiles appeared around a corner of the hallway and helped clear the way, and Cove instructed Theo over the bodies.

"The royals are in the drawing-room! The barricade's been broken!" one of the Exiles cried.

A roar went up around them.

Cove's stomach twisted hard. This was the result of a kingdom ruled by darkness for so long. A light was shown to the commoners and now, they would stop at nothing to chase more of it. Even if it meant violence and terror. Guards lay strewn, even some young maids and servants. Had they been killed indiscriminately? Or, in helping that young girl, had she helped a murderer escape? Certainly not.

She shoved the notion from her mind and turned to Theo. "Arne would be going to find where the royals are," she said. "Right?"

"Likely. Especially if he does not know Ingrid is here," Theo agreed. "But Ingrid is searching—and where Arne is, there Ingrid will be also. What about Bo?"

She surveyed the chaos around them, thinking. He had no bloodlust like the others did, and they had not made a pact to keep together once in the castle. So where...

"Right...there," Cove said, spying the man with his staff, knocking the legs out from under a guard. She chuckled despite herself. "Holding his own across this room."

"Good. Let's go?" Theo asked.

She steered them closer. "We'll have your back," Cove shouted to Bo, and he looked up only to nod. They formed a triangle, quickly attracting more guards with swords drawn. Cove cut two down, and Theo slashed with his dagger, landing another man dead to the floor. Bo's staff was just as deadly when driven at unguarded, soft throats.

"The fire! The fire, it's spreading!" a cry went up. "Retreat!"

"But the royals," Cove shouted. "Some of our people went after them!"

"Leave them!" someone shouted as they ran.

"We need to get out," Theo said. "Cove, you'd run the fastest. Get Arne and Ingrid and go!"

Cove scoffed. "I'm not leaving—"

Bo grabbed hold of Theo's arm. "I won't let him go this time. Do you trust me?"

His eyes bore into hers. *Did she?* Panic spooled around her throat and lungs.

Theo nodded his reassurance.

Before she could think, she spun on her heel and ran up a maze of stairs, until the smoke was intolerable. Commoners and guards alike were fleeing, screaming, running, falling, tripping over one another.

"Arne! Ingrid! Get out!" she called, over and over, in the hopes they might hear her. She'd found Bo and Theo on her own. Er, Theo had found *her*. Ingrid had called out to Cove before. She would find them again. She had to.

A hand shot out, grabbed her by the neck, and slammed her into the wall.

"*You*!"

Erik.

She didn't speak. Didn't move. Didn't breathe. He was hurt, one arm clearly dislocated. Blood poured from a head wound. Another in his leg. Was he dying?

He angled his face into hers, seething. "Because of you, the king will die. Because of you, the people woke up. All because of you..." His grip tightened on her neck.

"I can't claim any of those successes on my own. But because of *you*, I found peace," she choked out. "Go ahead. Kill me, Erik. I'll only get to see the man who saved me."

Rage turned his face purple. "Well, I'd hate to disappoint!" he sneered.

Erik fumbled for his sword. *Good*, Cove thought. So he really was going to end her life. But she was glad...at least now, she knew her fate was secure. The white tendrils racing up her arms seemed to warm her from the inside out. She would be all right. Theo would be, too, somehow.

Blood spewed across Cove's face, and the man gave a single expression of shock before he dropped to his knees, fingering the tip of the sword protruding from his stomach. He fell off to the side, dead.

A commoner simply nodded as he ripped the weapon from Erik and kept running.

Overwhelmed, Cove threw up before she frantically pawed the blood from her face. Her ears buzzed, and she pressed a palm to the wall to force herself upright.

He was gone.

"Arne! Ingrid!" Cove shouted, then choked. Her throat rasped.

"Here!" Ingrid's voice came again.

"Get out! We have to leave, now!"

"We're coming!" Ingrid was dragging Arne, who was walking backwards shouting insults.

"They're—"

"Staying?" Cove asked. "The royals. Are they staying?"

Ingrid pressed her lips together. "They seem to believe their altar here is..." She shook her head. "I don't understand it. It's more important to them than life itself. We have to go. Arne, please!" she shouted. Cove grabbed his other arm and towed. Finally, he snapped out of it and scrutinized Cove.

"Cove, you're—"

"It's not all my blood," she cut him off short, gesturing widely for the stairs. "Now, run!"

FORTY THREE

Cove

After escaping the chaos in the Citadel, Bo guided them to an underground tunnel, where they and several other Exiles stayed for two days until another person came and retrieved them.

"The fighting has ceased. The castle is in ruins. The king has been exposed," one of Iosua's students, Yon, said as he greeted the Exiles coming out of the tunnel. "Cephas sent word and said we would find you here."

"Has it been...troublesome aboveground?" Arne asked.

Theo tucked Cove under his arm, and she leaned into him, studying the man who they had broken bread with just days before.

The man puffed out his brown cheeks, exhaled slowly, and nodded. "Yes. But it is good. We needed this. It was planned regardless of whether Iosua..." He trailed off, his voice cracking. "Whether or not he sacrificed himself for us, the kingdom was going to fall."

Cove dipped her head. As much as she mourned Iosua's passing...it would have been torture for his men.

Ingrid spoke next. "The king...?"

"He was arrested. With no sacrifices and a refusal to follow El Elyon, they expect him to die in custody. Erik, his son, was killed as he attacked a young woman"—Theo's arm tightened around Cove—"and a troop of zealots took the opportunity. They went out to his manor to capture the rest of his family—all the brothers. They will be arrested and tried." He shook his head, and he stared far off as he mulled over something else. "We told the zealots to spread the word that the curse has been broken, as they move through the towns. The leader of the zealot order intends to cast lots to establish a new governance here." Again, the man paused. Finally, the ghost of a smile twitched at his mustache. "And there is more, but I believe it will be better discovered on your own."

Cove blinked. "What do you mean?"

His grin only brightened. "Have safe travels, Cove. We will see you again, I imagine. Take the most direct roads home and do not fear your capture. Should you encounter any guards who have not heard the news yet, they will soon learn."

Cove nodded slowly, more confused than ever. And with that, it was over.

Smoke still hung over the Gold Quarter, plaguing the air that she had once admired as clean. She turned toward Arne and Ingrid. "The rest of us have to go to the Red Quarter. But you...?"

"To my mother's, to collect the children." Ingrid beamed, though it was tense. "I wasn't sure we would ever get there. We still don't know what happened with Rune...with the information he shared. But I want to see my babies."

"We will travel with you," Bo announced. "Through the Gray Quarter, and then the Red. I am positive Cove can help Theo get where he needs to go?"

Cove wasn't certain *where* he belonged now. It was something they had discussed at length during their time in the tunnels. He didn't know what to do, and neither did she; not until they got out into the world. Even still, it would take time. With the king out of the picture, would Theo still be considered a scarlet letter, a cursed creature? Would he be disowned after word spread about the cure? The ruler was gone, but people were still superstitious. Ingrid had explained that it could take generations to dismantle the web of lies which had prevailed for centuries. And his parents...

"I want to go to them," Theo murmured, as if reading her mind. "My parents. Tell them about Iosua."

She shook her head. "Theo, they might..." *Hurt you. Threaten you. Disown you again.* She couldn't stand telling him what she feared.

"I know. But I have to try. Wouldn't you?" he asked. "Especially now?"

She'd told him of the intricate white pattern that coated her tan skin now. How it lay against her like lace, whiter than snow, pure. Not a threat of death, a candle drawing down to its nail. Now, she bore the picture of hope. She bore the semblance of a candle burning in the darkness.

“Of course. I plan to talk to my parents when we get home, too. I’ll go with you,” she assured him.

“Good, because I don’t know how I’d get there otherwise,” he said, a smirk creeping up his face.

She shoved him gently. “You’re awful.”

In all honesty, Cove was grateful to see a glimmer of teasing return. He’d been strangely silent in the aftermath, and she’d chalked it up to Iosua’s death, which she’d told him of after the dust settled and they were in the tunnel with nothing but time to spend. But there was more, wasn’t there? Questions left unanswered.

About her.

As they set out for the pathway, they moved with confidence through the Gold Quarter, talking with the teacher’s student Yon until the Quarter boundary, when he departed with a promise: more was still to come. Prophecies were still to unfold in the future, and Iosua’s sacrifice was only the beginning of life for him, not the end.

With the group in contemplative silence—how could death bring about life?—Cove dipped back to the end of the group with Theo, hoping to address his quietness from the past several days. “Are you all right, Theo? If your parents are concerning you…”

"It's not them," he said softly.

"Is it...me?" she asked. They hadn't spoken of his affections. Maybe he was waiting for her to speak up.

"No, of course not. I trust that you'll speak when you are ready. Either way." He paused, then continued. "Though I would appreciate a response."

She laughed softly. "If I tell you my answer, will you tell me what concerns you?" She reached up to smooth her thumb over his brow, which was wrinkled.

His face turned red. "Well, it depends on your answer..."

She swatted his arm, then kissed his cheek. "I have loved you since before I knew what love was, Theo. You've always been a part of my life. And now, I think we're free from everything that stopped us before. Everything that told us we couldn't pursue something together."

Wonder lit up Theo's face, but just as quickly replaced by that concern again.

"Unless you changed your mind," Cove added.

"No! No, of course not." He paused, sucking in a deep breath. "I love you, Cove. But...the curse was broken, and I am still blind."

He allowed their footsteps to fill the silence between them as Cove reasoned this. Of course, he'd been hoping that his blindness was a part of the curse. He believed his parents when they told him he'd done something terrible to deserve blindness from birth. They told him it was a curse, Iosua had promised a cure for the curse...but he was still blind as everyone else marveled in their ransom being paid. The curse was broken. And his hope, his fragile new idea of wholeness, was shattered. She had to be some kind of horrible, blind friend herself to not see that before.

"Theo..." Cove sighed. "I'm so sorry." She wrapped an arm around his middle, steered him around a dip in the cobblestones, then continued. "But you are not cursed by blindness. Your blindness is not because of who you are or what you've done."

"You don't know that."

"Of course I know. You're the kindest, most humble person I know!" Her voice rose with each word, though she didn't mean to shout. He wasn't deaf, after all. Just blind to his own worth just as much as he was to the world around them.

"Shh. Don't get them involved," Theo implored, nodding ahead to Arne, Bo, and Ingrid.

Their discussion had ebbed. She lowered her voice accordingly. "Theo...do you think I'm so disgusted by your blindness that I would reject you?"

"I'll never get to see you. I know you're beautiful, but I wish I could see it and tell you. And..." He trailed off. "Children, Cove. If we ever married...would they be blind, too?"

"Would I rather children who are blind but have the heart of a lion, or would I rather have children with the sickness of a duke's pride and perversion?" Cove asked. "They will learn from your heart, and I will tell you—and them—everything they need to see in this world. Whether they can see or not."

He fell silent for several moments. Finally, he mentioned, "You keep saying 'will' as if it's already done."

"Sorry, Theo, but I'm planning to keep you around," Cove said lightly, glad he couldn't see the way her cheeks blazed at her slip-up.

He grinned, though it still looked wary.

"Theo, I believe we need to have a discussion about how El Elyon sees you," a voice said behind them.

FORTY FOUR

Cove

Cove froze, Theo by extension. She spun around and gasped. "Iosua?"

He strode forward on the path, a knowing grin on his face, as though he'd been through this discussion several times over and was still amused by it. He wore a simple clean tunic and sandals, but his face radiated something bigger than it had before. Peace. Complete joy. Love. He held out his hands and she saw the holes where the nails had been driven through his wrists.

"You..." Words failed her. *You died. I watched you die. How are you here?*

"Cove, what's going on?" Theo's hand dug into her shoulder.

"It's...Iosua?" Her voice lilted up at the end, hardly able to believe it herself. How could she explain what she did not understand?

"Yes. Theo, it's me, Iosua." He raised his voice, glancing ahead toward Arne, Ingrid, and Bo. "You three! Get over here, please. I would like to speak with you."

The whole lot of them startled in shock, then Ingrid took off running and launched for an embrace.

Iosua caught her with a laugh. "Yes. Didn't I tell my disciples I would be back in three days?"

"But we..."

"Yes. I've been busy settling matters with them. But when they mentioned you were leaving...well, I have plenty of visits to make, and I decided to catch up with you quickly before you left." He took a deep breath, looking Theo up and down. "And I am glad that I did." Turning to Cove, he lifted his brows.

Cove stepped back, letting go of Theo's arm, and Iosua took Theo's shoulders, standing in front of him.

"Theo...you have been blind since birth, yes?"

Theo nodded silently.

"What could have caused you to sin before you were born, when you were yet in your mother's womb?" he asked.

"I-I don't know," Theo stammered.

"Nothing could have caused such sin, Theo," Iosua corrected him gently. "And there is nothing you could have done to deserve blindness. Do you believe El Elyon to be so unjust and cruel as to curse you himself, though you are his creation and beloved?"

Theo began to tremble beneath Iosua's touch, but he shook his head. "I am sorry, Iosua."

"No, it is because you have been told so your whole life, and because you have accepted it for so long. Child, you are not cursed, nor are you a burden. In this world, afflictions will still come upon people. Hurt still exists until eternity, when we escape sin and death once and for all. But El Elyon knows and grieves when such afflictions arise, and he knows and grieves with your heart when it grieves." Iosua laid a hand on Theo's heart, and Theo blinked rapidly. "Your blindness does not make you less of a person. It does not make you less worthy. It does not make you less worth forgiving and saving and loving. If you were the only person on this planet, I still would have sacrificed myself for you. It was worth the pain to ensure my sweetest friends would experience eternity with me one day. I have to go again, soon, and I will begin preparing a house for all of you in eternity. You and many others yet to come." He moved away from Theo for a moment, but still kept a hand on his shoulder as he watched the others. "You, my students, and everyone still to come—I want all of you to tell the world of my sacrifice and return. I want you to speak life over the areas where darkness still reigns, so they may experience freedom as you have." His gaze lingered on Cove, and a smile crept up over his cheeks. "I believe you will have no trouble doing so. Yes?"

"Of course," Cove said, nodding. "Thank you." She was impatient to get home to her mother and grandmother, that they might know the truth and be set free by it. Whether they accepted it or not, she wouldn't know. But Iosua opened her eyes to something more, too: what if she could tell more people?

A hushed chorus echoed her as the others agreed to tell...everyone. Then, Iosua turned back to Theo. "What a powerful testimony you, especially, will have. It is one thing to see and believe. It is another entirely to not see and still believe. And you have done so with your whole heart from the beginning."

He kissed the top of Theo's head, then let go and gestured for Cove to return to his side. She did quickly, lacing her fingers with Theo's. He squeezed tight.

"Will you walk with us? Perhaps you will head southeast with us?" Bo asked.

But Iosua shook his head. "I need to move on, and others are expecting me for the dinnertime meal." He paused. "Solmere will face many struggles in the coming months. But birthing pangs are necessary for new things, and I wish to see this kingdom brought to my Father. It is beyond time, hm?" he asked, and their heads all bobbed in unison. "So I will see you off. I love each of you completely."

Cove's mind raced with all of the things she'd wanted to ask him. All of the grief she'd tucked back. The confusion about her father appearing and disappearing. Why she was worth saving at all. Iosua met her gaze, and as if reading her mind, he said, "Some mysteries are meant to be explained in heaven. Remember, it is better to believe than it is to see."

She took a deep, shuddering breath and nodded. "Thank you." They exchanged pleasantries and I-love-yous once more, then they watched Iosua leave.

The pathway seemed brighter where he trod, and Cove's gaze was drawn downward. Where Iosua had walked, tender shoots of grass sprung from between the dirty gray cobblestones.

Life would return to Solmere once more.

FORTY FIVE

THEO

WALKING CONFIDENTLY THROUGH THE boundaries between quarters felt wrong, but Theo followed Cove and the others as they did just that. Sunlight shone down on his face and warmed his bones, and his mind dwelled on the length of time when there had been no sun at all. Bo explained to the group that the sun had disappeared because of Iosua's death. All of creation had mourned the loss of its creator sent to earth. Arne, Cove, and Bo...they had been there.

He wondered if that was what changed so drastically Cove. Why she walked with a more confident air about her, not scuffing her shoes or lagging behind with fingernails clenched into his shirt.

It was all laid bare between them, now. Bo and Arne had run out to help Cove, and Ingrid had run in to help the students get Iosua out safely—but they had stumbled right into Rune's own trap. And Rune...he shook his head. He'd heard the shing of Rune's sword as he and Ingrid had fled. Neither he nor Ingrid had spoken of it.

Goodbyes were shared with Arne and Ingrid on a path just before her mother's home, and there had been a flurry of embraces, kisses on cheeks, and assurances that Arne and Ingrid would keep in touch with Theo and Cove from now on. There was much work to do, and they would be part of it. Arne had clapped Theo on the back.

"Take care of 'er, now that you've got 'er," Arne said in his ear.

"I haven't got her just yet," Theo protested.

Arne had laughed. "Let those who have the gift of sight make that judgment. Believe me, brother. Trust me."

And then it was just Bo, Cove, and Theo.

"We'll reach home by this evening, Theo," Cove told him. She'd already promised that Bo could stay with her family overnight, before departing for his travels to the edge of the Red Quarter. So it was almost over. Their fellowship would be ending soon. And Theo still didn't know where he would belong.

His insides flopped. "Do you think I should talk with my parents?" he asked. "Maybe they won't even answer the door."

"I think you need to try. Like you told me before," Cove said. She squeezed his hand reassuringly. "I'll be right here, and Bo too."

"But what if they won't listen?"

"If they won't listen, you will have at least tried." Cove took a deep breath. "I know you, Theo, and I know it'll eat at you until you try."

He nodded, though he didn't bring up that he had nowhere to sleep, if they turned him away. Perhaps he could go on with Bo and live with the Exiles. Though he wasn't sure how far away the Exiles lived from Cove. Would he be able to leave her? Or go back to the Black Quarter and live where he knew how to navigate? Which would be safer?

As the sun slipped away for her nightly slumber, Cove squeezed his hand again. "We're almost here. I'll be right there with you. I promise."

"I will be, too," Bo promised. Theo felt a hand on his other shoulder.

"Thank you," he said. "I appreciate it. Both of you."

"Of course."

"Where else would we be?" Cove asked. She laughed. "What?"

"Saving you from the prison is what launched us into all of this. Do you think I'll abandon you now?"

He shook his head. "I don't even know how many siblings I have."

Bo hummed. "It is a dreadful day when a family breaks asunder and will not acknowledge one another. Something El Elyon said could happen, but he does not like to look upon such circumstances. It could be that your parents will not hear of your testimony, either."

"I know." Theo's voice trembled and he cleared his throat.

"But their acceptance of you, or lack thereof, doesn't bear knowledge of your worth," Cove said. "Hear me?"

He nodded, though he wanted to disagree with her. Deep inside, he wasn't sure he believed Iosua's words. And somehow, that ate at him too.

He lifted his knuckles and knocked three times. A commotion ensued, expletive-laced shouts filtering to the outside as his mother and father argued and a cacophony of young voices squabbled. Finally, the door creaked open.

"What'cha doing here?" a youngster asked.

Theo knelt. "Hi, there. What's your name?"

"Eileen."

He smiled. "Hi, Eileen. I'm here to talk to your parents. I'm..." *Your brother? Your family?* "I want to tell you about a friend of mine who broke the curse over all Solmere."

"Is it the king?" the little voice asked.

He faltered. "Yes...he's a king, but not the kind you're thinking of," he said. "The king who rules over all the world, not only Solmere."

"Get out of there, Eileen!" a voice shouted. Mother. Stomping feet came closer and then froze.

Theo rose to his feet in a hurry. "Mother?"

"How did you find your way...Cove. Of course." She cut off short. "Thought that girl would be dead by now. Who's the old man?"

"I am Bo. I am a priest with the Exiles. And your son has a good many things he would like to share with you about why 'that girl' is still alive." From Bo's tone, Theo could tell he didn't appreciate the way which his mother had appraised them.

His mother sniffed. He felt the spray of spittle landing near his feet, but he wouldn't shuffle backward. "My eldest son is dead."

"No, he isn't," Cove argued. "Don't say that! Just let him tell you what he has—"

"He's not welcome here. Who knows what curse might come upon us! Do you want to hurt your little siblings?" her voice was directed back toward him, and he resisted the urge to back up away from her.

"I thought you'd want to know that the curse is broken over our kingdom. Over the world. Hearts no longer turn to stone. El Elyon and his son, Iosua, have vanquished it from the land. You—"

She snorted. "Listen to you! You sound like an ill man. Get away from here and leave my children alone."

"But you'll die without knowing Him!" Theo blurted, taking a step forward.

"I said, go away!" she shouted. "You're still blind, aren't you? What curse has been lifted? Surely not yours! It is not safe for you to be around my children! Do you want them blind, too?"

The door slammed so hard he felt the wind on his face.

Cove's hand came up on his shoulder, then turned him slowly and guided him into her shoulder. "It's all right," she whispered into his ear. "They're wrong. You are perfect and whole as the person El Elyon made you to be."

He shook his head—but then Bo laid a hand on his back. "Don't disagree with her, son. She's right. El Elyon made you just so. We might not understand why, but it is not your fault. It is not a curse. It is you, and Iosua loves you. So do I. So does Cove."

Cove nodded, and he finally wrapped his arms around her, holding her tight, somehow wishing he could stuff Bo into their embrace too.

A gasp ripped through the air and tore them all apart. "Cove?"

FORTY SIX

COVE

"MOTHER?" COVE ASKED. SHE pulled Theo away from the door and gestured for Bo to follow. From the doorway of the cottage she had grown up in, several yards off from Theo's family, light poured from the fireplace. Her mother stood with arms crossed, and her grandmother peered over her mother's tense shoulder.

"You're not dead? We thought you..." Mother pressed a fist to her mouth and turned away.

"I'm all right. I'm alive," Cove called. She forced her feet to move quickly, murmuring instructions to Theo. "There's a dip in the ground here, and step over the roots..."

"I can take him," Bo offered.

"No," Cove said firmly. But then she cast a glance over her shoulder, realizing how she sounded. "Thank you, Bo. But I...I need him next to me as he needed me for his own confrontation."

Bo nodded in understanding. "Should I stay back?"

"No. I promised you lodging, remember? They'll be all right with it," Cove promised. *I'll make sure of it,* she added silently. Goodness only knew what Mother would say after she heard...everything.

The doorstep arrived too quickly. She let go of Theo only to pull her mother into a fierce embrace, but Mother fought against Cove.

"You don't get to come back after I spent days mourning you! Erik's men were here and they—"

"I'll tell you everything if you give me a chance. Can we come in?" Cove asked.

She let her mother go, and for the first time, her gaze swiveled to assess Bo standing at Cove's right side. "Who's he?" And then her brows wrinkled. "Theo? How are you here?"

He smiled. "That's part of Cove's story."

Grandmother piped up. "We've got tea on for the evening. I believe you need it more."

"Bo and Theo, yes," Cove said. "I'm all right." She knew full well they hadn't enough hot water for any more than that.

"I'll put on another pot," Mother said brusquely, dashing at her eyes as she turned away, heading for the tea. Grandmother quirked a brow at Cove.

"Come in, please," Cove said to the men, tucking her hand in Theo's elbow. She guided him to Mother's chair and let him sit, then asked Bo to take Grandmother's rocking chair. Grandmother harrumphed, but took a kitchen chair instead.

Mother's hands trembled as she offered the hot drinks to Bo and Theo, then nailed her gaze on Cove. "Explain yourself. Now."

So the story unfolded: how Theo had turned up missing. How Cove met Iosua. How she had to leave without telling anyone, because she knew Erik's men would come looking.

"I always hated him," Mother spat.

"He's dead now," Theo spoke up.

After her jaw dropped open, she remained silent for the rest of the story. Cove explained her doubts. Her uncertainty about who Iosua was, and how she was prepared to die as a sacrifice. Mother shook her head but said nothing. And then the death. The battle. The fallen king. And the return of Iosua, just recently.

"This has been in the works for centuries," Cove said, "since the beginning of time. Bo is an Exile priest, a man who studied the ancient texts and prophecies, which were hidden away when the king took reign and began destroying the texts."

"Is that true?" Mother asked Bo.

He nodded. "I can answer any questions you might have, ma'am. Just as I have done for your daughter and Theo."

Grandmother pointed a gnarled finger at Cove's fingers. "Your stains. They're white. Not black. What's that for?"

"This is what happens when you accept Iosua with your heart and mind." She rolled up her sleeves and tugged at the neckline of her dress. Mother and Grandmother gasped in unison, and Mother reached out to trace the white.

"What...what does this mean?" she asked in a low voice.

"The stone heart will not take me. I have been made pure by Iosua's sacrifice. And he can do the same for you. Right this moment. I was imprisoned when my stains turned white," Cove said, leaning forward. She was knelt on the floor before Mother, looking up. "And there's more that you need to know. Father did not die from the stone heart."

She shook her head and scoffed. "Of course he did, Cove, you—"

"He didn't, ma'am. I witnessed his murder. He was bringing me food and got caught by the guards. They said to tell you it was the stone heart because of his stains," Theo spoke up, and Mother's gaze flew to his face. He searched a corner somewhere to the right of Mother, and her gaze returned back to Cove.

Her eyes were clouded over with emotion."What does this mean?"

"It means we were lied to." Cove wanted to blurt that Mother had browbeaten her for her entire life over a death that hadn't occurred as she predicted. But it was done, it was over with, and it wasn't of consequence now. Cove knew the truth.

Would Mother seek the same?

"You learned all of this from Iosua," she murmured. "And..."

Cove sucked in a deep breath, about to blurt that she'd seen Father, so fleetingly, before the raid on the castle. But something stirred within her, speaking that it was a symbol meant only for her. So instead, she said, "Yes. Bo can tell you much about the prophecies. I offered him lodging for the night, as he will be travelling tomorrow."

"And what about Theo?" Mother asked. "Does he have a place to stay?"

"No." Cove bit her lip. "Could he..."

"In the living area, with Bo. By the fire. Yes. For tonight." She glanced over the boy. "Your family was wrong to turn you out."

"I worry more for their other children than for myself," Theo said.

"For good reason," Mother said grimly, then turned to Cove. She reached for Cove's face, cupping it in her hands. "I've spent my life blaming you, fearing you would end up as your father did. You're so strong-willed. But now I see...it was wrong of me to treat you so harshly. Will you forgive me?"

Cove nodded. "Yes, Mother. I forgive you already. It hurts, yes, but I don't want bitterness in me ever again."

Mother's face contorted. "I'm sorry. I'm so sorry. I thought you were dead."

She pressed her forehead against Cove's, a gesture that rocked her back to childhood. Before everything fell apart. When Mother would rock her to sleep and sang most of the day through. When she was soft herself.

"Will you talk to Bo?" Cove asked. "Please? And Grandmother?"

"Yes." Mother nodded. "We will. I promise."

With that, she rose quickly and announced that she needed to prepare the living area for Bo and Theo to rest in overnight.

As Cove trailed behind her, Theo caught her arm. "Is she upset?" he asked quietly.

"No." Cove rested her hand on his shoulder. "No, this is only how she reacts when emotions knock on her doorstep," she said with a wry grin.

"Perhaps your father isn't the only one you take after," he replied, eyebrows lifting.

"You..." She cut herself off short and shook her head. "With that, I must bid you leave."

"Like I said," was his teasing reply, which put Bo and Grandmother into a fit of rusty chuckles.

"I'll get the blankets from the linen closet," Cove announced as she drifted past Mother. She knew the woman had only gone to the kitchen to dry her eyes and collect herself, so she didn't want to intrude.

Instead, Mother sniffled and chuckled. "Theo, hm? It sounds like you two are still close."

"He loves me," Cove admitted quietly. As if the admission would break whatever trance they were all in.

Mother turned around, leaning against the counter and crossing her arms over her stomach, a small smile playing over her weary face. "I knew that from the start. Do you?"

Cove allowed herself a small nod. "He protected me on that whole journey. He never lost hope, never lost courage. He was willing to die protecting me from my own foolishness. He corrects me when I'm wrong."

Mother's eyebrows flew up. "The boy's brave."

"And he's right." Cove laughed. "Yes. I do love him. I know the village shuns him because of his blindness, but Mother, it's not his fault, he isn't cursed."

"I know that. Nobody that gentle and humble could be cursed by anything. Any demon who dared to would be struck dead by their own shame," Mother said. Finally, her lips curled upward in a tender expression Cove hadn't seen in over a decade. "If he were to offer you a life with him, would you accept it?"

"In an instant. We discussed it on the walk home, but—"

Mother's smile broadened. "Even through the hardship? You'll have to work, and he'll need your help. You could stay here, of course, but it's quite cramped."

"I know it will be work. But it will be worth it," Cove said quietly. "I'm convinced it is so. I just...haven't told him that yet."

Mother swatted her arm, faux-gasping. "You're letting that poor boy hang on thin air!"

"We've had a few more pressing matters to concern ourselves with," Cove argued in her defense.

Mother shook her head, the glimmer of tears still in her eyes afresh as she reached her arms out. Cove slipped into them. It had been years since her mother had offered up an embrace, and it felt unfamiliar. But still, she did. Rebuilding their relationship on a solid foundation would take time, she reminded herself. But it would also take willingness.

"I love you, my dear girl."

"Love you too, Mother."

EPILOGUE

Cove

Three months later

Cove sat next to Theo, softly describing her simple dress to him, guiding his hand as she described the lace at the collarbone, the simple, rough white linen for the bodice and skirt, and the tiny berries in her hair, which she'd foraged for earlier that day. They tucked her untamable curls behind her ears and formed a crown around her temple.

Once she was finished describing her gown, he took her hand and pressed the knuckles to his lips, kissing them softly.

Arne and Ingrid had taken Theo into their home while Cove gained a job doing laundry, repairing her reputation in her village and working to tear down the biases between the Red and Black Quarters. The new king and queen had ascended just a month ago, followers of Iosua and fair in their rule. They had immediately demanded that all Quarter barriers be taken down. It was Solmere, the kingdom of light as it had always been intended, not a kingdom split into quarters. Greenery grew back into the Gray Quarter, according to Ingrid and Arne, who had brought their children to the field beyond Cove's home for the special day. Ingrid had taken Cove aside before the ceremony to announce that she and Arne's next child would arrive in the summer.

The first generation to live in a new kingdom.

Bo had gone immediately to help grow the numbers of Iosua's followers, and tomorrow he would be departing on a ship for another country entirely. But by his eternal credit, he waited until Cove and Theo had agreed on a date to be wed. He was the only one either knew of who could marry them in El Elyon's sight.

And so, Cove had become Theo's wife roughly half an hour ago, and now she and Theo reclined against a tree as she described all the merriment. Arne and Ingrid's family danced in the meadow. Mother and Grandmother joined them. A few new friends, ones Theo had met in the Gray Quarter, had joined them on the journey. A few of Cove's clients joined them, bringing a feast for dinner, which Cove was anticipating.

"Come over here, you!" Ingrid called, coaxing Cove toward the dancing with a wide gesture.

Cove laughed, waving them off. "I'd rather watch."

"Oh, come on! Teach Theo how to dance with you!" she called. Her children ran over, grabbing their hands and pulling them into the fray. Cove and Theo laughed together, and he took her into his arms.

"You'll have to tell me," he chuckled.

"Of course." She didn't know the dance herself, but watched Ingrid's neat footwork. Ingrid noticed, and began calling out directions to her children, raising her voice and tossing a wink

Cove's way. The footwork seemed far too complicated for Cove's mind, but Theo quickly picked it up, moving hesitantly but correctly.

As they swept around the meadow, and rounded near Cove's mother's cottage, a set of small children trotted down the road toward them.

"Can we join?" a little girl asked. Eileen, as a matter of fact.

"Of course!" Cove called. "Come, come. And eat!"

"Is that...?" Theo asked softly.

"Mm-hmm. Would you rather visit with them?" she asked. The children hadn't seen Theo since their mother rejected Theo and forbade them to speak with him, but they had been to see Cove quite frequently. Most days, she found them trotting along at her heels as she went about her work through the village, having been turned out of the house for the day. She tried to help them when she could, sneaking food to them like she'd done for Theo. Like her father had done—the good her father had done. He was not always a good man, but he was not always a cruel one either, and Cove could learn from the good and the bad in equal measures. Arne had promised to help build a cottage next to Cove's mother, for Cove and Theo. And Cove secretly hoped those children would keep coming over despite their parents' hatred. If their parents could not see...perhaps their children's eyes could be opened instead.

It was worth trying. As the dance ended, Cove led Theo toward his little siblings.

"I'm glad you came to celebrate with us," she told them. "Do you want to visit with my husband?" They'd agreed not to tell the children that Theo was their brother, but rather, only Cove's beau. It would keep tension—and retaliation—to a minimum. They eagerly came over to Theo, asking him questions. He knelt, and the youngest, a little boy who could toddle at best, crawled up into his lap.

Theo tipped his head back toward Cove with a smile that could outshine the sun, and she ruffled his hair, kissing his forehead. "Can you tell us the story about Iosua?" Eileen asked. "Cove already told us. But she said you had more of the story."

"Did she, now?" Theo asked with a grin. Cove knelt beside him.

"Yes, I did." He kissed her cheek, then took a deep breath. "Well...it all began when I was kidnapped one day."

The little ones gasped, and soon enough, Ingrid's children raced over, drawn by the other young ones' attention.

Cove could envision a scene much like this in the coming years, when Theo's little siblings and Ingrid's could play and learn alongside Cove and Theo's own children. A place where they could frolic safely in the meadow. They would learn why Cove's arms were stained black and turned white, and about the man who sacrificed everything to make it happen for her...for them. They would learn why Theo was not broken, but whole in his own fearfully-created way, and how to love the ones their kingdom looked down on. And perhaps one day, Solmere would learn a kinder way. One generation at a time, taught of a conquered shadow and bearing the light that broke forth soon after.

AFTERWORD

THIS BOOK WAS AN undertaking. A form of storytelling I never tried before: allegory. Writing the world through eyes that cannot see. Dismantling and exposing lies that *so many* fall into, relating to pride and unforgiveness. It's hard stuff, but so worthwhile. In case you were unsure before, this is an allegory for the death and resurrection of Christ. *Iosua* is, of course, intended to point us toward Christ. It is something that pleads for eyes to be opened, hearts to be made new, and for softness to prevail in a world where pride and bitterness is made popular.

And so...

This book was written for the folks who struggle to be their own person with the shadow of abusive family behind them—or looming expectations. You can change. You can be different and grow and be whole in Christ. It is only through Christ that you will find what you're searching for, my love. I encourage you to try. To seek Him. To lay your stains at His feet.

He loves you so much.

This book was also written for those with chronic conditions. You are made with a beautiful purpose. You are a miracle. Your worth is in Christ, not what others say. You are so loved. I hope you find that love and family like Theo did—your tribe of supporters.

I wrote this book for the sinner coming home. The prodigal. The one seeking to *be* someone. I wrote this for Christ. For those who look in the mirror and see someone they don't like. If you are holding this book, you are holding years of prayer that this would lead you into a renewed, deeper relationship with Christ.

You have a choice to grow.

You have a choice to hold onto hope.

You have a choice to find the ones who love you in this world; the ones you will love likewise.

You have a choice to seek the One who loves you most of all.

He can turn those old stains white, just like Cove's stains. He loves you dearly. Your abilities do not define your worth; only He is capable of that! Rest in those promises today.

ABOUT THE AUTHOR

MICHAELA BUSH is a Christian author, editor, and entrepreneur. She graduated Magna Cum Laude in 2019 from Clarion University of Pennsylvania, where she earned a B.A. in English and a minor in Psychology. She has enjoyed writing from an early age, and mostly writes Christian fantasy and romance. When she isn't working or creating her next story, she enjoys spending time with her family, horseback riding, playing violin, and spending time at church. Follow her @tangledupinwriting.

IF YOU ENJOYED CONQUEROR OF SHADOW AND LIGHT...

PLEASE CONSIDER LEAVING A review on Goodreads or Amazon! They are so important, and so deeply appreciated, by authors!

www.ingramcontent.com/pod-product-compliance
Lightning Source LLC
La Vergne TN
LVHW100522110826
845146LV00002B/736